WHAT ARE FRIENDS FOR

WHAT ARE FRIENDS FOR

Michael Estorick

Brian & Arthur

who have seen it all before!

with love

Michael

London
June 25 1990

Duckworth

First published in 1990 by
Gerald Duckworth & Co. Ltd.
The Old Piano Facory
43 Gloucester Crescent, London NW1

ISBN 0 7156 2344 3

British Library Cataloguing in Publication Data

Estorick, Michael
    What are friends for
    I. Title
    823.914 [F]

ISBN 0-7156-2344-3

Photoset in North Wales by
Derek Doyle & Associates, Mold, Clwyd
Printed in Great Britain by
Billing & Son Limited, Worcester

For David Risner

Part One

1

I was crying, and for the life of me I didn't know
why. I'd been to funerals before, family affairs at
which, uncomfortable in a suit, I'd watched in
astonishment as my parents and their Middle-
European relations – the women in fur coats and
feathered hats, the men unshaven – clutched one
another and wept extravagantly. On such
occasions I don't know which had embarrassed
me more: their unself-consciousness or my
reserve. Now, in contrast, I was anxious only that
my outburst shouldn't be misconstrued, particularly by Jamie, for my tears were as conspicuous
in church as my reticence had been out of place
on those earlier occasions among fellow Jews.

Don't misunderstand me. It wasn't a question
of religion or faith. No believer in God, I'd long
forgotten all the Old Testament rigmarole I'd
been force-fed for my *Barmitzvah* twenty years
before. But one thing I'll admit to having had in

common with Duncan, apart from friendship with Jamie, was that we were both lousy at admitting to our emotions – though had it been my funeral instead of his I'm damn sure he'd have been in the forefront of mourners and not skulking at the back like me, ashamed of any show of feeling. Duncan always loved to draw attention to himself.

Duncan Ritchie had wanted to be all things to all men. Trying to lead as many lives as he had different faces, he'd lived in manifest terror of getting his wires crossed. On the morning of his funeral it was obvious that the mourners were divided by more than just the aisle in which his coffin stood. At last faces could be fitted to names, characters from conversation and correspondence be fleshed out. Of the many emotions I felt in church that morning curiosity was by far the least equivocal.

Jamie had sent printed directions and I'd arrived with time to spare. The wide suburban road was packed with cars, mainly fancy foreign jobs, and I had to park some distance from the church, after which I sat for twenty minutes with one eye on a newspaper and the other on the people arriving. As they slowly went past I recognised a number of faces. One or two acknowledged me. No one smiled.

I waited for the clock to strike the hour before going inside. By leaving it to the last minute I was hoping to avoid all the muttering and nodding and gazing at nothing in particular which fills the time before such occasions and an urge, hard to contain, to talk about Duncan which I knew would be frowned on, especially by Jamie. After being handed an order of service I found an empty pew near the back – near enough to hear what was being said, but not too close to draw anyone's attention.

I was astonished by the number of people who'd bothered to turn up. Duncan had never been popular – 'an acquired taste', even Jamie admitted – and it seemed a measure of the impression he made that so many people should have taken time off in the middle of the week.

Almost as soon as I sat down I began to feel jumpy, imagining everyone was staring at me, but fortunately just then the vicar climbed into his pulpit and we were off, and I realised I was only expressing my anxiety about being there at all. Though we'd known each other for ten years and spent a good deal of time together, Duncan and I hadn't exchanged a word in the weeks preceding his death. Nor after what he'd said had I had any intention of doing so again.

Typically, Jamie made light of what he called our 'tiff'. 'How many times have I heard that before?' he'd said, and when I insisted that Duncan had finally gone too far he'd put a hand on my shoulder and told me not to be 'so emotional' – a gesture which made me feel both petty and patronised. He'd added that I should be big enough to forgive the odd stupid remark, for wasn't it obvious it was only nerves that made

Duncan blurt out the first thing that entered his head?

God knows who Jamie was trying to convince. Even he wasn't disingenuous enough to believe that jokes about the concentration camps could be easily laughed off. By me, to use a favourite expression of my father's, Duncan could take a running leap. In the event I hardly expected him to take me literally.

After reassuring us that the hereafter was a better place than the here-and-now, the vicar was replaced by the editor of the newspaper for which Duncan had worked, who droned on about himself for a quarter of an hour – an ingenious and novel way of avoiding the pitfalls in eulogising as controversial a character as Duncan.

Duncan's boss resumed his seat and Jamie had begun to do his bit when I was distracted by the sound of someone trying to get in. Accompanied by angry voices, the noise increased until it was no longer possible to pretend that nothing was happening. Heads began to turn and there was an outbreak of coughing. Jamie, aware of a disturbance, began to falter and then stopped speaking altogether. Meanwhile someone in a cassock hurried, skirts billowing, down the aisle and heaved open the heavy wooden doors to admit a woman dressed from head to foot in black. She clearly had no idea where she was or what she was doing, and after wandering about the back of the church she was helped into the nearest pew, which happened also to be mine.

Close up, it was obvious she was smashed out of her head. Drawing back a veil to which bits of food and cigarette ash were stuck, she looked blankly about and then proceeded to empty the contents of her handbag onto the seat between us. She didn't seem to be looking for anything in particular, and while she examined each object in turn she slipped off her shoes and began to rub her toes. Then, aware that I was staring at her, she peered up and grinned. For what remained of the service I found myself unable to pay attention to anything else.

Afterwards, for no particular reason, I waited till the place was empty before going outside. The Black Widow, as I'd come to think of my neighbour, had dashed out as soon as the doors were open and before I'd had time to say a word to her, leaving behind an assortment of book matches, coins, make-up and a large, scrumpled handkerchief.

A number of people I knew by sight were standing round the porch in groups of three and four, lighting up, whispering, evidently reluctant to make any move before anyone else, no doubt keen for it all to be over so that they could get back to town and into more comfortable clothes. No one seemed in any hurry to be at the wake, least of all the Black Widow, who, at some distance from everyone, was squatting on a gravestone, smoking a roll-up. Bumming a cigarette, I looked around for Jamie.

For days I'd been looking forward to Jamie's

eulogy, but in the event I'd missed almost every word of it. Still, from the way people were pumping his hand he'd evidently produced the goods. While trying to think of something to say, I wondered how he'd have behaved if it had been my funeral. Jamie played his cards close to his chest, but something about the way he was carrying on reminded me of the triumphant candidate in an election. When he was at last alone I offered my congratulations.

'Mazeltov,' I said. 'That seemed to go down a treat ... better than your last effort, anyway.' Jamie couldn't fail to be aware of what I was referring to. As best man at a mutual friend's wedding six months before he had delivered a devastating speech – not, as one might have expected, in its wit or charm or generosity, but in its calculated rudeness to, of all people, the groom. Although Jamie was a notorious mickey-taker, one of the things I'd always admired in him was his instinct for knowing how far to go. On that occasion his judgment had entirely deserted him and, because I'd seen them laughing together beforehand, I was convinced that Duncan had put him up to it. Jamie always liked a challenge, and it wasn't hard to imagine Duncan offering the kind of inducement he'd find hard to resist.

Bob Rosen, my oldest friend, was not the only person to hold a low opinion of Jamie. He called him a *Luftmensch*: literally, a man who lives on air. But I could think of others, not least Duncan, to whom it applied with far more justice. In any case, Bob was hardly a reliable witness. He drank even more than I did and had suffered too many disappointments, both private and professional, to be free of envy. But I won't deny that the frostiness which seemed to enter my friendship with Jamie after the wedding was at least partly attributable to that disastrous speech. Overnight he seemed to have become dangerously unpredictable, and ready to turn on his friends for no apparent reason. Also, I resented the way one or two people who were justifiably upset held me responsible, on the basis of our known friendship, for what had happened at the wedding. Everyone must have known that Jamie never took anyone's advice on anything.

'Don't you ever give up?' he said, his eyes searching the churchyard for sanctuary.

'Considering Duncan's part in that fiasco I thought you showed admirable restraint today. I was hoping for some fireworks.'

'Dan, no one's laughing.'

'Nor was anyone at the wedding, apart from him, and he never could wait to see you make a fool of yourself. Still, I expect eulogies are as good a training for the aspiring politician as anything else.'

'Oh that,' he said, quickly looking away. 'I've given that up. To be precise, it's given me up.'

If true, this was a remarkable admission, and I said: 'Honestly?'

'Do you think I'd joke about a thing like that?'

'I'm just surprised. You seemed so sure of yourself. It's not like you to be easily discouraged.'

'I'd no choice. With more support I might have got somewhere, but no one seemed to want me. Except Duncan...'

'Yes, well ... if it's any consolation, I'm sorry.'

'It isn't,' he said.

Though Jamie was highly intelligent, resourceful and blessed with enormous energy, I'd never been able to take his politics seriously. Coming from a political family – both his father and grandfather had been long-serving Labour MPs – I shouldn't have been surprised when he announced his intention of standing for Parliament, but he could never convince me he was doing more than go through the motions. As a friend, it was ungenerous of me to feel pleased at his reversal, but I was relieved more for his sake than my own. Now that brief experiment had apparently come to nothing, I could at last look forward to his becoming himself once again.

While Jamie was speaking, he couldn't take his eyes off the Black Widow. Though hardly his type, she was attractive in a mad sort of way, and I wouldn't have put it past him to pick up someone at a funeral. When at last he turned back I asked him who she was.

'The one you've been ogling for the last ten minutes – the Black Widow,' I added, when he affected ignorance.

'Christ knows! She certainly doesn't know how

to behave.'

'I thought she added a bit of colour! Things were beginning to flag when she showed up.'

'Thanks very much!'

After a few moments' silence, he suddenly said: 'How do you know she's a widow?'

'It's just a figure of speech. She's probably some old slag of Duncan's.'

'I expect so,' he said, unconvincingly.

'But I thought he didn't like women?'

'He never stopped talking about them.'

'Still,' I added, 'you'd be sure to know. You're always making passes at your friends' girlfriends.'

'Don't be ridiculous,' he said and turned away.

As people began to leave the churchyard, Jamie suddenly became agitated. His eyes darted all over the place; he wrinkled his nose and blinked feverishly; then, without warning, he grabbed my arm. 'For Christ's sake, let's go. This place gives me the creeps,' he said, adding, as if expecting resistance, 'I'll explain in the pub. And do me a favour. No more of your lousy jokes. I'm not in the mood.'

It was the best part of an hour before I arrived at the Ritchies. I'd assumed Jamie was behind me, but by the time I found a parking space he wasn't to be seen. So, reluctant to go in on my own, I hung about self-consciously outside the mansion block, like someone planning a hold-up.

I'd certainly needed a drink. I may not be good at expressing my feelings, but I'm told I make my moods obvious to everyone around me, and I was anxious that my ambivalence towards Duncan shouldn't show in front of his family. From the little he'd ever said about them I gathered they'd played little part in his life. Perhaps he felt ashamed of his parents. Most children do at some time or other. More likely, he was embarrassed by some of his friends. He certainly never showed any sign of being ashamed of himself. My guess – and that's all it is – was that his family had refused to take him at his inflated self-estimation and were therefore dangerous to his amour-propre. Like so many people anxious to appear self-made, he'd gone to great lengths to stage-manage his life, but not even he could have dreamed up the sensational circumstances of his death and the world-wide publicity surrounding it.

Opposite the mansion block were some municipal tennis courts, netless and forlorn-looking, which recalled my first encounter with Duncan. I'd known Jamie then for a couple of years, and had been surprised when, a hopeless player myself, he'd asked me to make up a doubles at Queen's Club one Sunday morning. Jamie, slight, blond, blue-eyed, boyish, a little too pleased with his conspicuous physical attractions – 'The Hitler Youth', as I'd once jokingly called him – had worn cricket trousers and a silk scarf and was forever telling me good-humouredly where not to stand and what not to do, while across the net Duncan, in the briefest shorts and brandishing the most up-to-date metal racket, was forever charging towards me, stretching into his partner's court to volley, or hitting his second serve almost before a fault had been called. An irrepressible mixture of nervous energy and exhibitionism, he was like a toy which once wound up can't be stopped.

It was not that Duncan played particularly well – Jamie, a gifted mimic, did a wonderful send-up of Duncan getting overexcited – but he played as if his life depended on it, as if it was only by accident that he wasn't regularly hitting blistering passing shots, sending up tantalising lobs or weighing in with lethal smashes, because he was always trying so hard to do so. From the way he berated himself after almost every shot one might have thought he was having an uncharacteristic off-day, not, as I discovered in time, that he was playing as well as he ever would.

Afterwards, in the changing-room, Duncan had fatuously remarked in his booming public-school voice, that 'we must be about the only Englishmen in the place'. I didn't know him well enough to tell whether he was trying to be funny, but before anyone knew it a nasty scene had developed with an Italian-looking bloke who was getting ready to play. God knows what Jamie said to mollify him, but it was only through his intercession that Duncan got out of there in one piece. Later, in the bar, Duncan couldn't resist going over it all a hundred times, protesting total ignorance of what he was supposed to have said. By then, I was ready to clout him too, and it was only because of Jamie that we got any peace and quiet. On the way home I asked Jamie if his friend was always so obnoxious. 'Usually he's worse,' he said, laughing.

After ten minutes Jamie still hadn't shown up, so I took the rickety lift to the fifth floor and, after leaving my coat under a chair in the hallway, grabbed a drink and began to circulate.

A number of people were queuing to meet Duncan's parents, and I was on my second sherry when I found myself face to face with a tiny, over-made-up woman in middle-age, looking glazed. Before I'd time to identify myself, she said: 'I can't tell you how pleased we are to meet you at last. Duncan talked so much about you. One can tell you're an artist just by looking at you. Of course, he greatly admired your work. But then he regarded you and Jamie as his closest friends.'

There was something both pathetic and courageous about the breathless way she prattled on, a kind of sprightliness, less false than strained. I had an impression that she was astonished by the turnout, and worried that she hadn't catered for sufficient numbers.

It was just as well she did all the talking, for I was at a loss for words. What possible reason, I wondered, could Duncan have had for providing his parents with such a false picture of our relationship? And what distinguishing feature of mine had he emphasised that I should be so easily identifiable? My long, curving nose, curly black hair, French waiter's moustache? My off-hand manner, or habitual lateness? Perhaps the last. By arriving after almost everyone else, I had singled myself out. But I wouldn't have put it past Duncan to say something tactful, like 'He looks typically Jewish'. Mrs Ritchie finally stopped talking and smiled nervously. I then chipped in with a few well-rehearsed words and, before I'd time to put my foot in it, feeling a nudge from behind, squeezed her hand and quickly moved away.

Looking at the surprisingly large number crammed into that noisy, smoke-filled room, I was struck by the conspicuous absence of sadness. There was plenty to eat. Magically, my glass was always full. In next to no time I was feeling light-headed. All around me faces seemed to be smiling, and I began to understand something which had been eluding me: on such occasions no one had to justify, explain or apologise for his presence.

I must have recognised a third of the people, and every few minutes I found myself catching up on the details of someone's life. It seemed an appropriate occasion for re-establishing contact, for putting things as much as possible in their proper place. Duncan's death would affect everyone differently, force each to make his own

19

adjustments, but even so, the more people I spoke to the more perplexed I became. It was obvious that no one there had the slightest understanding of my real relationship with him, so much so that I began to wonder if Jamie's refrain, 'Of course you really like each other, you know you do' might contain some truth after all. Otherwise, it must have been obvious to Jamie that for years little love had been lost between us, that the abuse we heaped on each other whenever we met was no mere badinage; that it was only because of him that Duncan and I met at all.

After drinking steadily for a couple of hours I must have been pretty tight. I know that when, anxious for a spot of air, I stepped outside the flat the cold quickly made me dizzy and I had to hold the banister rail for support. Back in the drawing-room, I felt determined to clear up any misapprehensions about my so-called friendship with Duncan, and heard myself say things about Jamie, love, sex, money and ambition, which would normally have earned me a black eye, but which now only elicited sympathy. How far, I began to wonder, would I have to go to get a rise out of these chumps? What would I have to do to make them acknowledge the traitor in their midst?

By three o'clock less than half the mourners remained. Were they all by now as confused and befuddled as I was? Did no one else doubt why he was there? If nothing else, Duncan had provoked fierce responses in people; and it would have been incredible if I had been alone in feeling somewhat out of place.

I don't know what time Jamie had finally turned up, but he was now standing with the Ritchies, hands behind his back, head attentively inclined – grave, formal, respectful, solicitous – and a far cry from his usual engaging, extrovert self.

It had been from Jamie that I'd heard of Duncan's death, and I was at least grateful for that. Most people had seen it first on television or in the newspapers, and for them the shock must have been terrible. As a journalist, Duncan would have been gratified by the extensive coverage of his death. In other circumstances he would, no doubt, have been the first to jam his foot in the door to get at the grieving family; and, striving always for maximum impact, would have found in the publicity surrounding his own demise ample vindication for such an approach. The same could not be said for others. One thing everyone seemed to share was a revulsion at the way Duncan's death had been reported, at the gloating faces of those claiming responsibility, and the lingering shots of the burned-out wreckage of the helicopter in which he'd been travelling at the time.

Although Jamie was Duncan's best friend, I'd given little thought to what he must be feeling, for theirs was the intimacy of two similar people who give nothing of themselves away: a rhetorical relationship in which feelings and emotions are forever skirted because they are too terrifying to be approached head on. If, earlier in the day, Jamie had seemed almost to be enjoying himself, it must, I now realised, have been due only to nerves.

When Jamie moved away from the family I decided it was time to leave. We were by then among the stragglers, and the Ritchies, like everyone else, must have been feeling the strain of keeping up appearances. I went to the lavatory, and then to look for my coat, which had gone from the hall. When I found it finally in the bedroom, the belt was missing, and as I bent down to look for it I noticed on a bedside table a pile of library books and some unopened envelopes addressed to Duncan.

I suppose it was curiosity which made me pick the letters up, as if by holding them I was making contact with Duncan himself. They were mostly bills, typewritten buff envelopes with cellophane windows. And suddenly I felt angry. I was furious that they had been left there, and hadn't already been dealt with. Had I been more sober, I'd have been the first to admit I had no right to feel that way: at an appropriate time the letters would, no doubt, be answered; by placing them beside her bed, Mrs Ritchie had probably only been trying in some way to keep her son alive.

I was struggling to re-arrange the letters as I'd found them when I noticed in the corner of one of them the name of a life assurance company and, through the crinkled cellophane, the outline of a cheque.

The next thing I knew, Jamie was standing in the doorway, but I hardly noticed him, for I was sitting on the edge of the bed with my head in my hands, and tears pouring down my face.

2

Most mornings on my way to the studio I stop for breakfast at the Old Vienna, a seedy outpost of central Europe amidst the ubiquitous car showrooms and Chinese restaurants of the Finchley Road. Growing up in North London, the child of refugee parents, I'd heard about the 'Oy Vey', as my parents referred to it, for as long as I could remember. On Saturday mornings at the local Odeon, between *Goofy*, *Bugs Bunny* and *Look at Life* (remember *Leslie Mitchell Reporting*?) there would always be an advert for the place: shots of the rooms from different angles; towering plates of dumplings and red cabbage; a customer, napkin disappearing into his jowl, raising his glass; an old lady in a stupendous hat, force-feeding a defenceless brat. And when, twenty years later, I began to go there myself, it was exactly as I'd pictured it: none of the clientele seemed to have left their seats, the furniture and floral wallpaper had never been refurbished, or the Pyrex crockery replaced, and in the fancier dining-room which adjoined the 'coffee bar' the same sad-faced waiters in stained white jackets bent attentively over fragile old ladies with foreign accents.

Most middle-class Jewish kids from my part of the world know what it's like to be dragged off somewhere like the Old Vienna by cheek-pinching relatives and stuffed with chocolate cake; and, though my immediate family was small – just two parents, my sister and me – there always seemed to be someone – a crony of my mother's on her way to the hairdresser, a cigar-chewing client of the old man – happy to have me tag along for an hour or two while they *schmoozed* – so much so that, by the time I was *Barmitzvah'd*, I'd picked up a working knowledge of more or less every continental coffee-house and kosher restaurant from Golders Green to Wigmore Street.

Nowadays such old-world places are few and far between, but then each had its special character, a definite spirit of place, and even today some Jewish mother in diamonds and designer clothes comparing sun tans with her anorexic daughter will stick out like a sore thumb at the Old Vienna, though only a mile down the road among the brand-new BMWs and Mercedes she'll pass unremarked. The seediness – or lack of pretension, depending which way you look at it – is as much a part of the Old Vienna's charm as the goulash soup.

25

All such places have their regulars, jealous of 'their' seats and what they regard as their special relationship with the staff. But at the Old Vienna there is only one person to worry about. Whether shimmying about in a new perm or pair of black, patterned tights, singing out orders as if performing in opera or scribbling bills while her auctioneer's eyes scan the room for neglected customers and dirty plates – or, as often or not, neglected plates and dirty customers – Magdalena is the sun around which everything turns, and without which everything would be colder and darker. To her everyone, however old or ugly, is her 'Darling', 'Beautiful', or 'Baby', and forgotten just as soon as they've placed their order.

Usually I stop off at the O.V. on my way somewhere else, but when I haven't a class or can't face the studio I'll happily while away an hour or more, jealously eavesdropping on other people's conversation, leching after chain-smoking schoolgirls as they gossip about their boyfriends or, in the lull before lunchtime, surreptitiously sketching.

I've filled a half a dozen sketch books with people I've drawn at the Old Vienna: beetroot-faced deadbeats from the betting shops, devouring chips and the *Sporting Life*; heavy-lidded old gents, their chins supported by walking-sticks, staring into space; a bird-like woman energetically cutting up her husband's food; a gaggle of Jewish grannies, stabbing the air with bejewelled fingers and forkfuls of food as they natter about apple-strudel and Auschwitz. When I don't have to be somewhere else I find it hard to leave. There's always something going on, someone to watch or listen to; unlike *croissants*, time is one thing that never runs out.

On the Monday before Easter, six months almost to the day before Duncan's death, I arrived at the O.V. in a stinking mood, having ridden through a pothole in the People's Republic of Camden and buggered the front wheel of my bike. By then it was after ten, there were no *croissants* left, the only seat was in a draught beside the door; and even Magdalena seemed unwilling to acknowledge my presence.

Still, I had more important things to think about that day; for that matter we all did. Argentinian forces had just invaded the Falkland Islands, and I was loving every minute. Like a nymphomaniac, I just couldn't get enough of it. No sooner were the godforsaken islands in dago hands than I was sounding off in best backwoods fashion. I had all the answers: how the crisis would resolve itself; how this was going to be 'our' war; that every generation needed a war just as people had a duty to have children. At the Old Vienna, needless to say, one couldn't move for 'experts', deciding who was responsible and which heads must roll, where sovereignty lay and What Must Be Done; all the ifs and buts and hows and what it all did or didn't signify for Britain, NATO, Europe, the world, fascism, democracy, America and peace. On that historic Monday morning there was no position, however fatuous or uninformed, for which a taker could not be found, no aspect of the situation which, in the universal ignorance, some punter was unwilling to elucidate for the benefit of his neighbour or the room in general. In my mind's eye I could already see another instalment of Pathé News, could hear, above the din of voices and clatter of crockery, a British victory celebrated as only Leslie Mitchell, late of the Odeon Cinema, Swiss Cottage, knew how.

At the adjoining table three dapper old buzzards were at it hammer and tongs.

'Remember Munich?' one of them said, banging the floor with his cane.

'Who could forget?' said another, squeezing a cigarette into an ivory holder.

'They have. Believe me,' said the third, slowly rocking his head.

'And what about the Anschluss?'

'I was there.'

'We all were.'

'So we were! At my age it's easy to forget things.'

'Such things one never forgets!'

'This isn't quite the same,' the first man said, tapping out his pipe into a tin ashtray.

'So who said it was?'

'This *schnook* thinks it's the same.'

'*Schnook* yourself!'

I went for a pee. When I returned the three

were embroiled in an argument with someone at another table. I looked around. At every table people were hard at it, gesticulating with their arms, jabbing their fingers for emphasis, speaking either loudly or confidentially.

'The young these days! They know nothing.'

'They never did.'

'When I was a young man ...'

'Ancient history, my friend. Everything's changed. Today all they want ...'

'The man's *meshugga* that's all.'

'This place was always full of *meshugganas*.'

Too true, I thought, still trying to attract Magdalena's attention.

'What were you saying?'

'I wasn't saying anything.'

'You don't remember?'

'It can't have been important.'

'It sounded important.'

'Believe me, it was important!'

'Remember Budapest?' someone else said, to no one in particular.

'Now that was heaveeee!'

'Over one cup of coffee you could sit all day.'

'Without interruption!'

There was suddenly a lot of movement, and within moments the place was almost deserted.

'Magdalena?' one of the old buzzards called out.

'You can see she's busy.'

'He can't see anything.'

'But my coffee's cold.'

'Because you talk too much.'

Too true, I thought, my mind wandering. I gave the once-over to the pin-up in my neighbour's paper. She was definitely not worth going to war over. Then, chuckling, I thought: perhaps the old men are right and things haven't changed as much as we like to believe – once it was the War of Jenkin's Ear; now it was the War of Murdoch's Tit!

'Take Afghanistan,' a new contestant chipped in, drawing up a stool.

'You take it.'

'I don't want it.'

'No one wants it.'

'OK, what about Poland?'

'What about it?'

'Antisemites, the lot of them.'

'That's not the issue.'

'It's always the issue.'

'Of course Marx predicted it.'

'He predicted everything.'

'Another antisemite!'

'His father a rabbi, too.'

'Everyone's antisemitic.'

'That's for sure.'

'In the Falklands?'

'And why not?'

'But they're only sheep.'

'So what's new?'

Next to these characters I was a hopeless amateur. Not for the first time I understood how for hundreds of years Jewish scholars had been content to spend their lives writing commentaries on the *Talmud*, and commentaries on commentaries: something about angels dancing on the head of a pin ... Fumbling in my pocket for change, I got up to leave.

'You read what Levin wrote in *The Times*?'

'Who has time to read?'

'I can't even read the number on the bus.'

'Anyway, journalists are all the same.'

'Like politicians.'

'Only worse.'

'Right on!'

'Magdalena ...!'

When I got to the studio the phone was ringing, a shrill, nagging noise like the proverbial Jewish mother: not unlike my mother for that matter. At first I didn't recognise the voice. The caller either had a cold or was drunk.

Then Bob said: 'Guess what your great friend Duncan's done?'

'That shit's no friend of mine,' I said.

'Bollocks. You'll make it up. You always do. You want to be liked too much. That was always your problem, Dan.'

'At least no one could say that about you.'

I'd known Bob Rosen all my life, but first thing on a Monday he was more than I could take. So I said, 'I've just walked in. If it's important get it off your chest, otherwise I've work to do. Call me later if you like.'

'So now the great artist is too busy for his old

friends! Dan, this is your old mate Bob. Remember? Not one of your high-falutin' friends. Someone who remembers you when you were little Danny Cohen, not Dan Cowan, honorary goy.'

'Very funny,' I said, crushing a fly which was ambling across the table. 'What do you want?'

'Guess.'

In an effort to get rid of him I said the first thing that came into my head.

'Don't tell me, he's off to the Falklands.'

There was a furious outbreak of coughing on the line, followed by a brief silence. Then Bob said, 'I suppose that shit Wilkinson told you. The Task Force! I ask you!'

'You're joking?'

'Do I sound it?'

'I can no longer tell.' Then, picturing Duncan prancing through sheepshit, I began to laugh.

'It's all over Fleet Street,' Bob added.

Realising he was telling the truth made me suddenly angry, and I said, 'Why can't he watch it on TV like everyone else?'

My words were greeted by a loud clattering, followed by a string of four-letter words and more coughing. At last he said: 'You don't imagine we're going to invade a godforsaken lump of rock in the middle of nowhere?'

'I've been thinking of nothing else.'

'It'll be Suez over again. As soon as things get serious the Yanks'll step in.'

'It's serious already,' I said.

'Five minutes ago Thatcher was all set to take away their bloody passports, now she wants to send a fucking armada.'

'What's that got to do with it. Remember Munich?'

'Don't give me that!'

'But we have to show we mean business.'

'Why? They're not going to invade us.'

'That's not the point,' I said.

'Then what is?'

I rested the receiver on the table to light a cigarette and give myself time to think.

'Isn't it enough that British lives are at stake?' I said finally.

'Only if Thatcher goes on making stupid threats.'

'You think the Argies give a shit about the islanders? Christ, they don't care about their own people. How many have disappeared in the past few years? Ten thousand? Twenty? Fifty? If you'd listened to Saturday's debate, you'd know she hasn't any choice. It was like the kill at a hunt: everyone was baying for blood.'

'Yes, well, you'd know more about that than me.'

'Next you'll be saying you want to go too.'

'It's the opportunity of a lifetime,' he said.

'I don't remember seeing your by-line on too many scoops from the world's hot-spots, unless you count Balmoral and Sandringham. Anyway, if you're so keen to go, I'm sure your paper can arrange it.'

'You don't understand. The bastards don't want to take anyone.'

'Why do you care anyway if nothing's going to happen?'

'Too many people have a stake in seeing this thing through. Tory politicians, the military/ industrial complex ... Not even you can think it's come out of the blue. Why do you think *Endurance* was withdrawn, if not to invite an invasion?'

'That's preposterous.'

'Then how do you think they got all those ships ready in time?'

'Quite frankly, I hadn't thought about it,' I confessed.

'Precisely!'

'Anyway,' I said, 'if that's true, surely you're better off here, leaving the dirty work to the pros. It's what a professional army's for, after all.'

'Oh fuck,' he said, 'you just don't understand.'

A minute or two later Bob was back, wheezing heavily. Then he seemed to disappear. Then there was a clatter, suggesting he'd dropped the phone, and he was gone. When, almost immediately, the phone rang again, I snatched up the receiver.

'What the hell is it now?' I said. 'I'm busy.'

'Daniel! Is that any way to speak to your mother?'

'I thought you were someone else.'

'You talk to other people like that?'

'Only to friends.'

'Friends?'

'Mum, it's really not important.'

'You use such foul language to your friends?'

'I was joking.'

'Joking?'

'Mum... what is it? I'm very busy.'

'Too busy to speak to your only mother?'

'OK, what do you want?'

'By me it's enough you should keep in touch. But since you ask, we were wondering which day you were coming for dinner?'

'Which day? You haven't even asked us.'

'Whenever you like. Tonight, tomorrow?'

'I can't. I've a lot on. I'm very busy. Anyway, we came on Friday, only three days ago.'

'It seems longer.'

'Well, it isn't,' I said, hoping that was an end of it.

'So what shall I tell your father? You know he'll be disappointed not to see you.'

Like hell, I thought, and said, 'Say whatever you like. Tell him Janet's working nights. Anything.'

'Come without her.'

'I'm teaching.'

'Every night?'

'Yes,' I lied. 'Every night. So if it's OK I'll call in a week or so and we'll fix something up.'

'A week?'

'Yes, Mum. Seven days. OK? Now I've got to run. Talk to you.'

Hardly had I put the receiver down when it rang again.

'Lunch is out too,' I said, snatching it up.

'Even with me?' asked Jamie.

'Not necessarily. What are you offering?'

'Why are Jews all the same, always trying to make a deal?'

'Very funny. Tell me, what's the futures market in mothers?'

'Buy long – sell short. As always!'

'Don't I know it!'

'How about today,' he said, 'at the Club, about one? I've something to celebrate.'

'Why didn't you say so?'

'You didn't ask.'

'So why don't you Goys ever say what you mean?'

3

I was a few minutes early arriving in Pall Mall and, after chaining the Raleigh to the railings, waited in the street for Jamie. A stream of impeccably dressed men strolled into the building, each of whom made me feel self-conscious in my old cords and hacking jacket. It wouldn't have occurred to Jamie to warn me what to wear – he probably imagined everyone went to work in a suit. The only club I knew was where my parents played bridge, and people indistinguishable from the regulars of the O.V. spent their afternoons enveloped in cigarette smoke, drinking tea and abusing one another. With its ponderous neo-classical facade and grand, dimly lit rooms visible across a stone balustrade, Jamie's 'gentlemen's' club seemed forbidding in a quite different way – the sort of place in which old buffers dozed in front of blazing fires and never addressed a word to anyone.

How such places survive is quite beyond me: packed full of the upwardly-mobile or people like Jamie who, as they say in France, live on the right and vote on the left. No doubt, I'd be better placed to see their point if, like him, I'd been to public school, or had clients to entertain. For years he'd been banging on about how life in England was just an extension of school, and having met a few of his friends I was ready to believe him.

After standing in the cold for a quarter of an hour it occurred to me that Jamie might be waiting inside, so bracing myself I wandered up a few stone steps and through the hallowed portals.

I should have guessed that Jamie wouldn't be there, nor had he left any message, and it was twenty to two when he finally turned up, by which time I was ready to leave the dingy waiting-room to which I'd been consigned by a snooty doorman in shit-coloured livery.

'Sorry,' Jamie said, smiling unapologetically, 'the old man wanted a talk and you know what that means. He was hoping to join us, but with this flap on ... it's playing hell with everyone's arrangements.'

'I'm sure the Argies wouldn't have invaded if they'd known,' I said.

We knocked back a couple of large ones; then, at Jamie's suggestion, took our glasses with us to the dining-room which was about to close. On the stairs he turned to me and said, 'Wild tie! Only wish I could get away with that myself, but you know how stuffy the City is. It sounds ridiculous, but in my position I'm expected to dress not to offend others rather than to please myself.' Peering at the eyesore round my neck, he added, 'That must be a collector's item by now.'

'It was all they had at the door,' I said. 'It never occurred to me I'd need one.'

'No, I suppose it wouldn't,' he said. 'Well, don't forget to leave it when you go.'

'You don't think I'd be seen dead in it anywhere else?'

We were shown to a table in the large, panelled dining-room, dimly illuminated by a domed skylight, and after the waiter had taken our order Jamie leaned back in his chair, swallowed the remains of his drink and said, 'I must say, I'm feeling pretty pleased with myself.'

'I can see that.'

'It isn't official, but I'm at last going to be made a partner in the old firm.' He paused for a moment while I muttered my congratulations and then went on as if I hadn't spoken. 'I'd been expecting it of course. *Franchement*, the old man's a bit past it. If he'd any intention of handing over the reins, it only made sense to get a move on.'

Glancing round the almost empty room, he leaned forward and, in a whisper, added: 'I'd been putting it about, discreetly of course, that the competition were casting an eye in my direction. Still, I must say it's a relief. In a business like ours there's always an outside chance some wide boy will come along and upset the applecart.'

In the dozen years we'd been friends, this was as much as he'd ever said about his work. The blatant contradiction in a self-styled socialist working in the City was too obvious to remark, especially as Jamie knew exactly what I thought of his politics. With no very clear idea what his promotion signified, I repeated my congratulations.

'Yes, well, thanks. As I say, it's a weight off my mind.'

'Why? It can't come as much of a surprise.'

'No, of course not, but one can never be sure of these things, especially in a firm our size. The speed everything's changing in the City these days, it's sometimes hard to keep up. One minute you think you're in control, the next it's slipped through your fingers. You wouldn't believe the pressure I'm under.'

'No,' I said, 'I don't expect I would.'

At that moment the wine waiter appeared and after slopping a little wine into Jamie's glass looked on superciliously while my friend went into a routine I could hardly believe. First, he swirled the wine around the glass. Then mumbling what sounded like 'Good Legs', he held it to the light. Then he pressed the glass to his face. Finally, when there was nothing else to do, he tasted it.

I found it hard to keep a straight face while this was going on. There was something so portentous and self-important about Jamie's behaviour, one would have thought he'd just been made Chairman of the Board. Was this the same devil-may-care friend I'd known and loved for a decade and more? A little fatter perhaps, but otherwise hardly changed? When a few moments later Jamie spoke again, I realised I was consciously reappraising him. 'You didn't mind my choosing?' he said, 'there are a couple of things I've been able to persuade the wine committee to order. Usually, they're very stuffy. Only the other day I heard some old bird call St Emilion 'half way to Burgundy'. I ask you! Sometimes it's like pissing into a howling gale trying to get them to wake their bloody ideas up.'

I smiled uncomfortably as I remembered all the times we had grabbed a bite to eat in some sordid South Ken *bistro*. A carafe or two of the house plonk had been quite good enough for him then.

'You'll never guess where it's from,' he went on, holding his glass to the light. 'Lebanon of all places. It's grown in the Bekka Valley and stored north of Beirut. When you consider how long the civil war's been going on and how the place has been carved up by warlords, each controlling his tiny bit of turf, it's amazing we get any of the stuff.' Masking his face with the glass, he inhaled deeply. 'Marvellous nose, don't you think?' he said.

'Marvellous,' I echoed. Then, making a feeble stab at humour, I added: 'That depends on what kind of nose we're talking about.'

'Oh,' he said, smiling, 'from the size it must be Jewish, wouldn't you say?'

We ate our first course in silence. When the

41

plates had been cleared away, I said, helping myself to more wine: 'Tell me, how do you square being a lefty with belonging to a place like this?'

'Don't tell me you're one of those people who think socialists shouldn't take holidays or ever enjoy themselves? Not everyone who's been to public school votes Tory, you know. Anyway, you mustn't confuse the clothes with the person inside.'

'I'm not sure I recognise him any more,' I said, rather to my surprise.

It was irritation with his superciliousness which had made me bring up politics, for we had agreed long ago that for the sake of our friendship it would be safer to keep off the subject. Jamie wasn't exactly Walter Mitty but, as his taste in clothes revealed, he was a great striker of poses – one minute the innocent prep schoolboy in his grey flannel suit, the next got up like a pantomime brigand in floor-length fur and trousers tucked into his boots.

At times I suspected Jamie knew when he was putting it on, but one couldn't ever be sure. Far from feeling concerned for other people or interested in building a better world, his socialist zeal was no more than a defence against admitting that he was different from the rest of his family.

'Next you'll be telling me the Labour Party was started by someone who went to school at Eton.'

'As a matter of fact it was,' he said. 'And all because he couldn't get into the Eleven! Still, you of all people should understand that.'

'Sorry?'

'As a Jew, I mean.'

'You know I don't believe any of that,' I said. 'If I'm anything, I'm an atheist. You know, a person with no invisible means of support. Or visible, for that matter, unlike you ... But I suppose what you mean is that centuries of oppression should have made me more sensitive and understanding of other people's suffering. That's crap, as far as I'm concerned. Rough treatment is just as likely to make you selfish and unfeeling. I expect the same's true of people who've been to boarding school. Look at Duncan.'

'I was referring to the Palestinians.'

'I know.'

'I expect you feel guilty.'

'Why? It was a Labour Government which created the Palestinian problem in the first place.'

'Past history,' he said. 'Anyway, I never said I approved of everything that goes on in the party. We're a broad church, and only a moron would swallow it all. But when it comes to the general outlines – public ownership of the 'natural' monopolies – gas, electricity, the railways – redistribution of incomes and the Welfare State, of course I do. Doesn't everyone, deep down?'

'As long as it isn't your income or your children

going to some inner-city comprehensive.'

Jamie, who'd never shown any interest in getting married and having children, had no answer to this, and after sitting in silence for a minute or two, gazing at nothing in particular and wondering what the hell I was doing in that gloomy place, I said: 'At least you know where you are with the Tories. They don't make any of those bogus distinctions between anti-Zionism and anti-semitism we're always hearing from the so-called anti-racist Left.'

I helped myself to wine. Though I'd hardly noticed, Jamie was right. It was delicious, and for a moment I forgot what it was I wanted to say. Then, making no attempt to keep my voice down, I said, 'My parents live in glorious, suburban, Finchley, which happens to be Margaret Thatcher's constituency. You may not know it, but her majority depends on the Jewish vote. And hardly a day goes by that my mother doesn't reel off the name of the latest Jew to have reached some or other high office. It's like a *brocha*, sorry, a grace before the meal...'

I began tossing out the names with which I'd become familiar since 1979. 'Keith Joseph, Lawson, Brittan ... how many's that?' I asked.

'Who's counting?' he said.

'You see, it's a Jewish trait to ask of someone before anything else: "Is he one of us?" Perhaps it's not surprising when Jews make up even less than one per cent of the population, only about a third the number of Moslems.'

'For an atheist you seem to know a lot about it!'

'You must admit it's an extraordinary achievement, in the circumstances.'

'No one's denying it. But if you're that keen to take the credit, you should be prepared to shoulder some of the blame.'

'Look,' I said, not wanting an argument, 'the point is, with success comes anxiety: what'll happen when things change? Not if – when. I don't expect you to understand, but if my father could see me now it would confirm all his worst fears.'

'No one here minds you're Jewish, if that's what's bothering you.'

'That's never been my problem. For some of us born after the war it's just history. Not the camps, of course; but at school, if someone made a stupid remark, it didn't amount to much. But to my parents it's just as real now as then. To them everything's the thin end of the wedge.'

'Dan, you know I don't care that you're Jewish.'

'Not as an individual perhaps, but tell me how many Jews are there in your beloved Labour Party?'

'How should I know? Plenty, I expect. Anyway, I'm sure you know them all by heart.'

'There's Gerald Kaufman,' I said. 'Who else?'

I don't know what had set me off. It was probably a measure of the discomfort I felt in that place; or, conversely, that Jamie seemed too much at home for my liking. I know he must have been wondering what he'd done to provoke such an

45

outburst.

'We have all sorts here,' he said. 'Christ, they're even thinking of admitting women, which is more than can be said of most clubs.'

I burst out laughing. Could he possibly have missed the point or was he just trying to change the subject? Either way, the ingenuousness of his response seemed to dissolve the tension between us which had been building up throughout lunch. Raising my glass, I said: 'This isn't getting us anywhere. We're supposed to be celebrating, not bitching like fairies.'

'Keep your voice down, will you?'

'Why? No one can hear. Anyway, no one would ever mistake you for a queer.'

'Look,' he said, reddening, 'times are changing and one has to move with them. Once I'm on the committee I'll be in a position to shake things up. A year from now you'll be asking me to put you up for membership, mark my words.'

'Not bloody likely! And anyway, why would you want to start changing the rules? They're what give these places their quaint distinction. Start admitting people like me and you won't be exclusive any longer.'

'We've got to raise money somehow. These places can't get by without fully utilising all their resources. There are whole floors on which no one ever sets foot. It's just not on.'

'You know', I said, smiling, 'when I close my eyes I hear the authentic voice of Thatcher's Britain.'

Apart from one old boy who appeared to have nodded off, we were the only people left in the dining-room. Jamie, however, seemed oblivious to any pressure from the waiters who were noisily clearing away and, tucking into his bread-and-butter pudding, said: 'I expect you've heard about Duncan?'

'You'd think he'd retaken the bloody islands single-handed, the way everyone's going on. Bob Rosen called just before you. He obviously feels he's missed the boat, in more ways than one.'

'Envy,' Jamie said, refilling first his glass and then mine, from a second decanter. 'Frankly, I don't rate Duncan's chances, but don't tell him I said so.'

'I thought it was settled?'

'That's what he thinks.'

'He's always been a damn sight too cocky.'

'It's not his fault. He's up against the Establishment. The last thing they ever want are newspapermen up their noses. Anyway, aren't you overdoing it a bit? I can understand Robert feeling pissed off, but why do you care?'

'Do I need a reason?'

He leaned forward and tapped the side of his nose. 'There was a pow-wow yesterday at the Reform, someone from the MOD trying to sort out journalists for the Armada. Stitch them up, more like it.'

'Isn't that where *Around the World in Eighty Days* began?' I asked.

'Duncan's been pestering the old man ever

since the trouble blew up, which shows how little he knows about these things. The services don't want to take anyone, of course, but even this government will have to allow token press representation. You've got to give him credit for trying.'

'He's always been trying!'

'Of course, none of this would have happened if they'd had the sense to take someone from *The Times*. But there was a ballot for places and only people from the *Sun* and *Titbits* got on, so they had to start again. I expect they baulked at the prospect of topless penguins on Page 3!'

'How the hell do you know all this?' I asked.

'When you've been around as long as I have there's not much you don't know about, and there's been a lot of excitement this weekend. Of course, the whole thing's ridiculous, but in my position I can hardly say so. Do you know, Michael Foot didn't even consult the Shadow Cabinet before speaking in Saturday's debate? Unbelievable!'

'You sound like the *Kama Sutra*,' I said, thinking of all the positions he was taking. 'Why do you think it's wrong to fight for what's rightfully yours?'

'We can't afford to, that's all. As for our much-vaunted rights, despite what's being said publicly no one's clear on that score. At best we acquired the islands by conquest from Spain.'

'Isn't that legitimate enough for you?'

'This isn't Palestine,' he said.

'Don't I know it!'

'If they're that confident,' he went on. 'Why've they been trying to get rid of the islands for so long? Because it's not practical to hold on to them, that's why. Gunboat diplomacy may once have been an effective way of getting shot of recalcitrant wogs. Nowadays the stakes are too high. People can't be allowed to go round starting wars just because they feel like it.'

'Funny, I seem to remember an Argentinian invasion. But my memory may be playing up. As they say, a week's a long time in politics. I wouldn't expect an old hand like you to remember that far back!'

'This isn't some playground squabble. What's important is to stop it escalating. Once the big boys get involved we've all had it.' Jamie paused to light a cigarette. 'Let's face it, Thatcher's popularity in the country is zero, the lowest of any PM ever, so she's got sod-all to lose by a bit of sabre-rattling. Think what it'll be like if she gets the Argies to back down, or if we actually invade. There'll be no room in the party for people like me, that's for sure.'

'Is that what this is all about?'

'If Michael bloody Foot hadn't opened his big mouth on Saturday there wouldn't be any Task Force. She'd never have had the nerve to go ahead. And he goes and gives her his backing without consulting anyone. Incredible!'

'Why are you getting so hot under the collar?' I asked. 'You're not still dreaming of becoming an

MP?'

'What did you think I was talking about?'

'But I thought you'd given all that up years ago.'

'Why? Nothing's changed, rather the reverse.' Jamie said. 'I still do my bit at elections, in the constituency, whatever I'm asked. A damn sight more, for that matter. I don't make a song and dance about it, that's all.'

'And...?'

'Nothing's been decided yet. Things are very fluid and I'm keeping my options open.'

'As the actress said to the Bishop!'

After lunch we moved into the library, helped ourselves to coffee, and found a table in a deserted corner overlooking St James's Park. After the wine I was feeling distinctly mellow, and at the back of my mind wrote off the rest of the afternoon. I also had the feeling that Jamie hadn't finished. Content as I was to celebrate his promotion, I couldn't believe it was his only reason for asking me there. Though vain, it was not in his character to go to great lengths to blow his own trumpet. And almost as soon as we'd sat down he brought up the subject which had first come to mind when he'd asked me to lunch. He said: 'I didn't see you in church on Saturday.'

'I hardly make a habit of it! If you hadn't been best man I wouldn't have bothered,' I said. 'But it was worth it, though it's beyond me how you had the nerve to say what you did.'

'I can't see why everyone is so excited. It was

only a joke. It's what the best man's there for.'

'He's not supposed to insinuate the groom's a queer.'

'But he probably is.'

'Even less reason.'

'How was I to know they'd be so stuffy? Christ, it was hard to think of anything to say.'

'Well, I'm glad I've never asked you to be my best man.'

He looked up quickly. 'Surely you're not thinking of getting spliced?'

'We've no immediate plans.'

'So you are thinking about it.'

'Why do you care? It wouldn't change things. Between us, I mean.'

'Don't be so sure. Anyway, you know I wouldn't make that kind of speech at your wedding.'

'I couldn't afford the risk. Since Saturday you've become a hot property!'

'For God's sake! It was only a stupid speech.'

'I always thought they were important to politicians.'

'Well, I'm not one yet, so let's drop it,' he said.

But I was beginning to warm to the subject, and said: 'By the way, what odds did Duncan give you?'

'It had nothing to do with him. It was just a joke. A damn, stupid joke. OK?'

I couldn't remember seeing Jamie so jumpy, but after the way he'd been laying it on over lunch, I was getting a kick out of teasing him.

Affecting a casualness he was obviously far from feeling, he said: 'I expect you've heard a rumour about Sally and me.'

Sally was the name of Saturday's bride.

'No,' I said. 'Why?'

'Someone's been going round saying I was trying to get my own back on her.'

'What on earth for?'

'I'm supposed to have proposed to her and been turned down. I ask you! Sally!'

'And did you?'

'What do you think?'

'You've been out with some dogs in your time.'

'I've never pretended I was going to marry them. Honestly, can you see me proposing to anyone?'

'Not unless you believed it was the only way you could get them into bed.'

'Have you ever fucked anyone that way?'

'I've never tried. I'd be too nervous they might say yes!'

'I do have some integrity, you know, in spite of what everyone seems to think,' he said, so solemnly it was hard to keep a straight face.

'Who do you think's behind it?' I asked.

'I wish I knew. The phone's not stopped all morning. I've even had the *Mail* on the line, trying to dig up some shit for their gossip column. If that happens, I can kiss goodbye to any chance of a seat.'

'It could be Duncan, I suppose.'

'Be serious.'

'I'm joking,' I lied.

'Good. Then can we drop it once and for all?'

'You brought it up,' I said.

'Good man.'

A flunkey appeared at Jamie's elbow to say he was wanted on the telephone. When he returned, he said: 'Talk about coincidence! That was Duncan. He's on his way over.'

'Have they surrendered already?'

'Stay for a glass of port? It's still early.'

'Better not,' I said, looking at my watch. It was ten to four. 'I might do something you'd regret, and I wouldn't want to muck up this fine old rug. Who knows, any day now you might need to sell it!'

'Sometimes I really don't understand you,' Jamie said.

'That makes two of us. Anyway, it's not just Duncan. I've a lot on.'

Jamie walked me to the top of the stairs, and indicated the way out. 'You're still OK for the weekend?' he asked, when I'd thanked him for lunch.

'Provided I've finished everything.'

'You can't drop out now. It's all arranged. Everyone's looking forward to your coming.

'I'll do my best,' I said, knowing nothing would stop me going.

'Great. And not a word about the wedding. To anyone.'

By now I was fed up with the whole subject, so I said: 'You may as well resign yourself to a little publicity. If I know Duncan ...'

'The little sod wouldn't dare.'

I put a hand on his shoulder and smiled.

'Oh, very funny!' he said. 'I can rely on you, can't I?'

'Mum's the word.'

'Cheers! And don't forget to leave that tie.'

4

The Wilkinsons lived a couple of hours' drive from London in a large, ugly Victorian rectory at the end of a long private drive – 'The Old Rectum. A very desirable gentleman's residence in parkland setting, with mature trees, paddock, ornamental lake, walled garden, granny-flat and "unusual" Royal Tennis Court,' as Jamie once described it, mimicking an estate agent.

When I arrived on the Thursday evening the house was in darkness. I let myself in and, after dumping my bag in the hall, followed the uncharacteristic sound of raised voices to the drawing-room. There was a row going on, but though the door was ajar I couldn't make out what was being said, only that Jamie's voice was the loudest; and when, during a lull and feeling rather like the detective in a whodunnit, I went in, found my friend pacing the carpet, while his father poured himself a drink and Mrs Wilkinson looked anxiously from one to the other. My arrival was evidently a source of relief more than embarrassment and in no time I found myself

alone with Jamie's brother. I'd known Simon for
years but we'd never had much to say to each
other, and when Jamie returned he left the room.
To my amazement, even before Simon was out of
the door, Jamie rounded on me.

'Where the hell have you been?' he said, pouring himself a drink.

I held out my empty glass and said, 'What was
all that about? It was like Hitler's bunker when I
walked in. You look half cut.'

'So would you,' he said, but when he failed to
elaborate, I said: 'You haven't been waiting for
me? You knew when I'd get here.'

'I told them but they wouldn't listen. They
never do.'

'It's a bloody miracle I'm here at all,' I said. 'I've
been at a piss-up all day. Then Janet kicked up a
fuss. Stupid cow didn't want me to come.'

'Perhaps you should have listened to her,' he
said, throwing his head back as if to say, You'll
never catch me being ruled by a woman.

'Very funny,'.

Normally Jamie was highly controlled, but the
few times I'd seen him lose his temper, he'd gone
right over the top. Something in his tone of voice
and constant fidgeting made me think this might
be such an occasion, so to sidetrack him I began to
describe the ritual end-of-term drink with my
students, a day of compelling awfulness which
had begun in the studios and progressed via an
assortment of sordid pubs to somebody's parents'
house. I embellished my account with exagger-

ated details of drunken students confessing to crushes on teachers and teachers feeling-up their pupils, but soon realised he wasn't listening.

'I wasn't doing badly for an old trouper,' I said. 'Then I saw the time. You know how it is.'

'You should have stayed.'

'I know.'

All of a sudden I felt a headache coming on and asked Jamie for a refill. He waved a hand at the drinks trolley, and said: 'Help yourself. This is as much your home as mine.'

'I was being courteous.'

'Like hell! Anyway, I'm not a bloody flunkey.'

'And I didn't drive a hundred miles to watch you have your period. Can't you see I'm trying to help?'

' "We're only trying to help. It's for your own good. We've only your best interests at heart." That's all anyone round here ever says when what they mean is: "Let us walk all over you." '

'Some people are turned on by it. Public schoolboys not unlike yourself, I'll be bound ... I'll be bound? Get it? It's a joke ... all right, I give up.'

'Every family needs a scapegoat. But it's not going to work. I've got their measure.'

'Really?' I asked. 'And who are they?'

Jamie stared at me, evidently trying to decide whether he trusted me enough to go on, and then turned away.

'Good try,' he said. 'But it's nothing. I'm famished,' he added, at last taking my empty glass.

'Your family's a damn sight nicer than mine, if

it's any consolation,' I said.

'Don't you ever give up?'

'Not with an audience as good as you!' I said, and fortunately just at that moment Mrs Wilkinson put her head round the door to tell us that dinner was ready.

It was after eleven when we finally got up from the table. Throughout the long-drawn-out meal everyone had been unusually subdued, no one more so than Jamie, and no reference was made to what had been going on when I arrived. Not that it was hard to imagine. With my parents hardly a meal goes by without some furious argument ending in a silent stand-off, but the Wilkinsons were nothing like them. In the midst of the most heated discussion they always remained respectful of each other, detached without being distant or wary, solicitous but never nosy or interfering. Nor did anyone seem to care if you disagreed with him. And if they were at times almost too ready to see the other person's point of view, making me wish that for once someone would lose his temper, there was something in that appearance of harmonious family life which was as comforting to me as it was foreign. That Jamie seemed put out whenever I addressed his parents – at their insistence – by their first names, was typical of his English reserve.

Perhaps at times I idealised the Wilkinsons, but they had been like a second family to me. Where my mother's extravagant claims on my behalf made me cringe in embarrassment, Mrs Wilkinson was quietly encouraging. Over the years she had helped me to find work, listened patiently to complaints about my philistine father and cloying mother, made me feel every bit as important as any Cabinet Minister or celebrity who also happened to be in the house. And if over the past few years Jamie and I had drifted somewhat apart – meeting as much as half a dozen times in a fortnight and then not for months – I never felt any less at home with his family – even though, as on that evening, the oasis seemed transformed into a mirage. But if I was upset at my exclusion I was also relieved. Despite all the thunder and lightning, in my own family I at least knew where I stood.

After helping to clear away, Jamie and I returned to the drawing-room. He had always been a night owl and I was beginning to get my second wind – light-headedness, probably, after the long drive mixed with relief that term was at last over – and I was in no hurry to call it a day.

Handing me an excessively large brandy, Jamie apologised for his rudeness earlier. 'It's not your fault,' he added, 'it's this place. I always look forward to coming here, but when we're all together I want to scream.'

'Be my guest,' I said.

'You know, my family really believe they're broadminded. My father spends most of his time trying to get the Official Secrets Act reformed. That dreadful catch-all Section Two which everyone always says must be got rid of but no one does anything about. More open government – it's what the opposition always want, of course, because they can't bear not having power themselves. But when he's with us the old man wants to know everything. He can't bear to feel out of things. It's the other side of the coin – if you know what everyone's up to there's no need to worry about secrets. Orwell was spot-on.'

'That's only normal,' I suggested, thinking of the complete lack of interest my father took in anything not involving himself. 'He's getting on, after all. At least he doesn't tell you what to do.'

'He wouldn't dare.'

'To him you're only a child, his little boy, and to you he's the omnipotent, larger-than-life figure from your childhood. Big Daddy, you might say.'

'Spare me,' he said. 'Knowledge is power. It's as simple as that. Anyway, since when were you so hot on psychology?'

'I'm not, but Freud was one of us – a Jew, I mean.'

'How could anyone forget?' he said. 'No, the truth is, he thinks because this is his house he has the right to know everything that goes on. Just look around. He's everywhere.'

Jamie couldn't have cared less if I agreed with him. I was a sounding-board, someone to bounce ideas and feelings against, or a mirror in which to see his own reflection. Of course, in a way he was right, one had only to look around to feel the omnipresence of his father: in the many photographs on the mantelpiece and desk, in the clutter of objects picked up abroad or presented for services rendered. No doubt he was to be found among the hundreds of MPs in the reproduction of the State Opening of Parliament which hung over the fireplace; certainly he towered over everyone in the wall-size family portrait done when Bratby and the Kitchen-Sink School were all the rage and Jamie still in short trousers; his name was handwritten on numerous engraved invitations and tooled in gold leaf on the spines of half a dozen leather-bound books shut away behind glass. But so what? It wasn't as if Jamie wasn't also there, eating with his family on the tree-lined terrace of their farmhouse in Tuscany, or seated cross-legged in the foreground of the family portrait; with cropped hair at prep school and long hair at university, or in helmet and goggles at the wheel of his Daimler Dart. After all, even I was represented in that room, by a pen-and-wash drawing of the house done years before which still brought a smile to my lips whenever I saw it.

'You're just paranoid,' I said, drinking it all in.

'And you don't know how lucky you are having a family that expects nothing of you.'

'You think it's so easy being Einstein and Mendelssohn and Horowitz rolled into one, when you can't even play the piano?'

'Don't be obtuse,' he said. But I wasn't at all sure I understood what he was getting at, and said:

'Look, all I know is, whatever I do is never as bad or as good as they expect. Which is a relief. It means I don't have to worry all the time about their good opinion.'

'Precisely! You're not under the same pressure.'

'What pressure?' I asked, piqued at his refusal to equate our situations. 'When were you last threatened with being cut off without a penny?'

'Money's got nothing to do with it.'

'You would think that!'

'Anyway, it isn't just this place, it's everything. Nothing ever changes because nothing's allowed to. It's always Mummy and Daddy and Lizzie and Simon and Jamie, but we're no longer children. Still, why should I expect you to understand? It's the British middle-class disease: terminal bloody adolescence.'

'You'd be livid if your parents decided to sell this place,' I said, 'though they're always saying they'd prefer somewhere smaller. Christ, they're only keeping it for you! And anyway, I thought you liked having somewhere you belonged. A lot of people would give their eye-teeth for a small part of what you've got, you know. I hate to tell you,' I added, 'but you're not that special. When it comes down to it we're all much the same. We want our parents to change but they're too old. And why should they if they're happy as they are?' I was thinking on my feet now. 'Perhaps that's what you can't bear,' I said. 'It's not that they expect anything of you, but what you still expect of them.'

Jamie looked distinctly uncomfortable and said: 'The country's just the same, the way it mythologises its past because it can't accept the present. If politicians had courage there'd be none of this Falklands nonsense. Even my old man, who has plenty of the right ideas, is a victim of the system. A conspiracy of silence militates against any possibility of real change. You're bloody lucky not having been to public school. Otherwise you'd know just how pernicious the class system is. At least you've had the chance to grow up among real people. Of course,' he added quickly, 'you'll say I'm romanticising the working class who are only a bunch of unwashed louts with rotten teeth who read the *Sun* and stab people at football matches, or that with their restrictive practices, trade unions are just a mirror-image of the Establishment. But if we were grown-up we'd be able to rise above all that. Regrettably, that takes imagination, a readiness to accept limitations, an awareness of difficulties, a willingness to shed the past, all of which only comes with self-knowledge.' After saying this, he glanced at me. Perhaps he was wondering how his wonderful words were being received. Then he said: 'You know I still can't believe my father's backing Thatcher over her bloody Armada, and dares to call himself a socialist. He can't even see the contradiction! I mean, if one can no longer rely on decent, old-fashioned sorts like him, what hope is there?'

This was all a bit much, especially coming from

Jamie, and I said: 'Did you make all that up or can you now afford a speech-writer?'

As usual, he was posturing, trying on a philosophical or moral suit in the same way I'd seen him try on clothes which he had no intention of buying.

'Anyway,' I said, 'you can hardly blame him. it isn't easy being a middle-of-the-road socialist these days. With no prospect of Labour getting in, people like him must be wondering what it's all for. You know that old chestnut about being a socialist when you're young and a conservative when you're old.'

'Read the polls. It's only a matter of time.'

'Don't tell me that's what you were getting so worked up about when I got here?' I asked. 'No one takes politics *that* seriously.'

'Unlike you, I happen to care what happens to this country. Anyway, you know my family better than that. We never argue. We just agree to differ. The trouble with you bloody arty types is you haven't the first idea about life.'

'Perhaps. But I still know bullshit when I hear it,' I said. And with that I decided to call it a day.

There was no one about when I came down in the morning, so I went into the dining-room to help myself to breakfast. It was already half past ten, but I decided not to wake Jamie. After the previous night's entertainment the last thing I fancied was spending a couple of hours twiddling my thumbs while he hid behind a newspaper groaning for attention and refusing to speak to me.

Everything was laid out on the sideboard, and I was helping myself to coffee and toast when I realised I wasn't alone. Seated by the window at the far end of the room was a blond woman wearing a green tweed jacket. To avoid alarming her, I loudly cleared my throat and she turned her head and briefly looked me over. Then she nodded, and without speaking went back to her book.

If there's one thing I can't stand it's a silly, stuck-up bitch treating me as if I don't exist. The art school I teach at is full of them: supercilious little dabblers with whining voices and rich daddies who try to get you to do their work for them while they sit around all day gossiping. I may not be as posh as Jamie, but I don't expect to be treated like a bloody serf. So when, on refilling her cup, I received barely a glance, I left the room, only to bump into Jamie in the corridor outside, dressed in a track-suit and standing on his head.

When he saw me, he returned to his feet, rose onto his toes and performed a daft pirouette. Then, humming, he began to wave his arms about.

'Let me guess. You're a tree. No, you're Gilbert and George ... none of those? I give up,' I said, going upstairs.

'Wait,' he murmured.

'Why? What is it?'

'Tai Chi.'

'Tie what?'

'Chi ... Chi. It means Great Ultimate ... in Chinese. It's an oriental form of non-violent self-defence,' Jamie added, coming to rest.

'Sounds more like the Labour Party!' I said. 'I can just see you all getting up at the party conference and swaying together to the *Internationale*!'

'Very droll. I always do it for at least ten minutes after my morning run. Clears the system. You should try it. It'll get rid of that flab.'

'So I can be like you?' I asked. 'Roll on Leni Riefenstahl!'

Jamie seemed miles away. Then, he suddenly said: 'What a fantastic day! Come and meet Lou,' and before I could stop him he'd taken my arm and was dragging me back into the dining-room.

The blonde didn't even look up when we walked in, but in his ebullience Jamie seemed not to notice and, after helping himself to coffee, he went and stood behind her chair. Despite his jaunty air there was nevertheless something contrived about his behaviour, and I wasn't surprised when, as he bent over to kiss her, she turned her face away. Immediately Jamie straightened up. Though his hand lingered on her shoulder, he was plainly furious. In an unnaturally loud voice he announced that he was going for a bath, but as soon as he was outside the room made straight for the drinks tray in the drawing-room.

'Silly bitch,' he said, as I closed the door. 'She's always showing me up in front of my friends.'

From this I gathered that he had known her for some time, but I wasn't surprised that he'd never mentioned her before. Jamie was pathologically secretive about his love-life and habitually went to ground at the start of an affair.

'She's probably shy,' I said. 'Whore in the bedroom, I bet.'

'Fucking prickteaser's more like it.'

'Anyway, I thought Jennifer was coming this weekend.'

'Something came up,' he said. 'Don't, for God's sake, mention Lou if you see her.'

'What do you take me for?' I said, angry that he felt the need to ask.

'I'm not used to being given the runaround, that's all. It makes me feel such a prick.'

'Tai Chi,' I said.

Jamie poured himself a drink and I asked a few questions – how long he'd known Lou and where they'd met, how old she was and what she did – but he seemed reluctant to discuss her and I decided not to press him.

Although he tried to mask it behind a devil-may-care manner, Jamie had always taken himself seriously. But recently he seemed to have lost any capacity to laugh at himself, preferring instead to make jokes at other people's expense. As we sat in silence I wondered what had become of wit and irony, the rapid-fire verbal pyrotechnics at which he was so adept, or the whimsical imaginative flights with which his conversation had once been filled to overflowing.

On recent evidence he had lost not just the capacity to laugh at himself but the capacity for laughter altogether.

After a few minutes, I realised he was determined not to move from his chair. Unable to stomach any more self-pity, I told him I'd see him later on and went upstairs to my room.

5

At Easter, by tradition, a curious event took place in a vast, chapel-like building a few hundred yards from the Wilkinsons' house, when teams representing the Houses of Commons and Lords played against each other at Real Tennis.

The match itself was little more than an excuse for a piss-up, and as far as I knew was almost the only occasion the court was still used. During the war it had been taken over by the army, and though efforts had since been made to patch it up, even the Wilkinsons, who weren't exactly short of a bob or two, soon realised they had a white elephant on their hands. But a preservation order stopped them knocking it down and the local authority had refused permission to convert the building into flats, so they leased it to a local farmer to use as a barn.

With its acres of mustard-coloured brickwork and filthy caged windows the building was a real Edwardian eyesore, a relic of leisurely days when the rich weren't ashamed to flaunt their wealth or indulge in harmless pleasures. Adjoining the court, in a large, wood-panelled room from which the game was watched, a few faded snaps of old players and house-parties hung on the damp walls, above bales of straw and rusting farm machinery.

The annual match was usually a great talking point among the Wilkinsons, but at dinner the previous evening it hadn't been so much as mentioned, and I assumed that it had been cancelled. Hence my surprise when, immediately after lunch, Jamie suggested we wander down to the court to see what was going on.

In the room adjoining the court there was the usual collection of old men in long white trousers with booming voices, calling out 'Well played' and 'Good shot' and 'I'm drinking red', and as soon as we walked in one of them button-holed Jamie.

'Just the chap we're looking for,' he said eagerly, and I could see from Jamie's face that already he was regretting our visit: 'Look here. One of our team has had to chuck – you know how things are at the moment, and I know you've played a bit – got a half-blue, if I remember – so if you've nothing better to do how about making up the numbers? Your friend won't mind watching, I'm sure,' he added, looking straight through me.

Louise had gone upstairs with a headache and we had nothing planned for the afternoon, but Jamie gave me the kind of searching look people make at parties when they need rescuing. I'd never seen him play, but I'd heard from various people how he'd won all these cups for games, and I didn't see how he could refuse, so I just shrugged my shoulders.

'I'd like to help out, of course', Jamie said, looking daggers, 'but we only popped in to see if you needed anything. We were on our way back to the house. Anyway, I've no kit.'

'No problem. I'm sure we can fix up something.'

'The thing is, much as I'd like to, I must get some work done. We've only just finished lunch, so I couldn't play for a while anyway. I wouldn't be able to move,' he added, chuckling insincerely.

'You wouldn't be on till three-thirty.'

'Won't it be too dark? You know how bad the lights are.'

'Look,' the man said, losing patience, 'if you really think you can't manage I'm sure Gerry will understand. It's a shame of course, he was adamant we could count on you, but we can probably fix him up with some doubles.'

'I'd be playing my father?' Jamie said.

'Didn't you know? The old boy's been banging on about it all morning!'

'Then I suppose that settles it,' Jamie said.

The game arranged, we settled down, drinks in hand, to watch what was going on. As I say, I'd seen Real Tennis once or twice, but I'd never got the hang of it. The floor was covered in different coloured lines. The players were forever changing ends for no obvious reason, and the language

71

it was scored in was Double-Dutch. Euphoria would break out whenever someone hit the ball into a panel at the far end of the court, or a bell was made to ring: shots whose significance was quite beyond me. But whenever I asked Jamie to explain, he seemed to think I was being bloody-minded, for he could never understand how anyone could fail to follow something which was obvious to him. Perhaps he was also getting his own back for my failure to come up with some excuse on his behalf.

When the match in progress came to an end hundreds of soggy-looking grey balls were collected up in a basket and a new game began.

While the players changed ends, Jamie said: 'Stupid old sods. I don't know why they bother.' And then, making no effort to keep his voice down, 'Fuck it. Why do I always let myself be talked into things?'

Some martyr! I thought, and said: 'It'll do you good, you'll get a kick out of beating him.'

'Why should I care? He's an old man.'

'All right, you don't want to beat him. Forget it.'

'No, explain what you meant.'

'It'd take too long.'

'I'm not in any hurry.'

'Well, I am,' I said, standing up to leave.

Jamie's match had already begun by the time I returned. Mr Wilkinson in knee-length khaki shorts, grunted as he lumbered after the ball, while his son, equally old-fashioned-looking in baggy cricket trousers held up by a striped tie, ambled about, nonchalantly returning everything which came over the net.

Then the players changed ends and Jamie served an ace which he repeated with the very next serve, to the accompaniment of jeering and laughter. In the next few minutes one game quickly followed another and the first set was soon finished. According to my neighbour, who sounded like an expert, the match was already as good as over. With luck there might still be time for doubles, he added, rather unfairly I thought, as he was supposed to be on Mr Wilkinson's side.

But then things began to change. Where earlier Jamie had only to hit the ball past his father to win a point, he was all of a sudden being made to run about, and after a couple of games even removed the pullover he was wearing.

From the way he pushed the hair out of his eyes and fidgeted with his racket-handle, I sensed that Jamie was getting flustered, but his very next shot was a peach which dropped like a stone in the corner, bringing gasps from the spectators and a cry of 'Good shot' from his father, and I realised that my neighbour was probably correct and it was only a matter of time before Jamie won.

Frankly, I was astonished at the ease with which he played – never hurrying, always seeming to be in the right place to hit the ball – and I felt almost as if I was seeing him at home for the first time. While Mr Wilkinson huffed and puffed his way around the court, Jamie was all elegance and ease. Whether stroking the ball from side to side as if he had it on a string, or deceiving his father with some sudden change of pace or direction, Jamie was as graceful and confident as a drawing by Matisse. Nevertheless, after a hard-fought final game, Mr Wilkinson somehow won the second set to resounding applause from everyone except his son.

Jamie was standing nearby when the final set began and, as he helped himself to balls from the trough at the back of the court, he winked at me. In that instant I found myself disliking him intensely. Though I didn't doubt he would win if he wanted to, I also had no wish to watch him humiliate his father and when in no time he was leading 4-1 I decided I'd had enough and went outside.

When I got back Jamie and his father were standing together with the spectators. Mr Wilkinson wore a towel round his neck and a broad smile on his face while he listened to people telling him how well he'd performed for a man his age. Evidently this was meant to console him, and I thought how typical it was of the English to congratulate a loser. But I was also relieved that Jamie wasn't hogging the limelight. And as soon as he went into the changing room I offered my congratulations. Without a trace of humour he said: 'Are you trying to be funny?'

'Sorry?'

'You saw what happened? '

'If you must know I was bored and went for a walk. No one would explain anything and you were having such an easy time of it. You won in the end. That's what matters.'

'Of course I bloody well didn't win. Do you think I'd be like this if I had?'

Surprised, but not entirely displeased, I said: 'Don't blame me. It was obvious you could have won if you'd wanted.'

'I don't give a damn about the stupid game. I know perfectly well I could have beaten him if I'd been in practice. Christ, I haven't picked up a racket in months. What I couldn't stick were all those pompous old soaks patting him on the back and telling him what a great chap he was. They take it all so bloody seriously.'

'That'll teach you not to fool around.'

'You don't think I take such things seriously? Games aren't real life, you know.'

'If I could play half as well as you I'd want to do it all the time,' I said, which was perfectly true.

'Yes, well, you're not me. At least I can see beyond the end of my nose.'

'That's only because yours isn't as large as mine!'

After his shower, Jamie stood like a statue in the middle of the changing room admiring himself. He had his back to me and was so absorbed in whatever he was doing that when I coughed he started suddenly and grabbed a towel.

'It's all right,' I said. 'I've seen a naked man before.'

'I don't fucking believe it. The stupid bitch has given me a dose!'

'That's no way to talk about the woman you love.'

'You don't think I'm in love with Louise, do you?' he said, turning round.

'I was referring to Jennifer. Anyway, I thought Louise was frigid?'

'She hates men, which amounts to the same thing.' Then, seeing my amusement, he added: 'You can laugh. You've probably had every form of clap in the book.'

'For God's sake! It's probably only over-use. Athlete's prick!'

'What if it's herpes? There's no cure.'

'It won't drop off over the weekend ... unless it's leprosy, in which case I'll give you a bell for Christmas!'

'What?' he said, glancing up. 'Oh, very funny.'

'Don't tell me you've never had anything.'

'I've always been very careful.'

'You mean to fuck anything that moves! Anyway, no one can be that careful. A woman can have gonorrhoea without even knowing it.'

'But what am I going to tell Jennifer?'

'Perhaps you caught it from her.'

'Be serious.'

'Jamie, no one would deliberately give anyone a dose.'

'It was Louise. I know it.'

'And if not?'

'Who else could it be?'

'How should I know? Ask Duncan. He's the one who keeps a record of all your lovers.'

'Very funny,' Jamie said, not realising that I wasn't joking.

Afterwards we strolled in silence back towards the house. I was just behind him as we went up to the terrace when he stopped so abruptly that we collided. But Jamie seemed hardly to notice me, and when I looked up I understood why. Only a few feet away Louise and Simon were sitting together on a garden bench. They were at opposite ends and faced away from each other, and in a public place would have been taken for strangers. However, to Jamie, convinced by now that Louise had deliberately given him an incurable disease, such proximity was evidently torment.

Normally, I would have expected Jamie to appreciate what was going on. But I was in no mood to humour him, and without waiting to see what happened, I mumbled some excuse and turned quickly on my heels, more relieved to be out of his company than I'd have believed possible even a few hours before.

6

At first I didn't know where I was or whether it was day or night. The light above my bed was dazzling, but the curtains were open, it was dark outside and I was fully clothed. The last thing I remembered was lying down with a splitting headache, but that might have been hours before. When I turned to look at my watch on the bedside table, I saw Jamie's mother standing in the doorway, looking distraught. 'Please come downstairs. Something terrible's happened,' she said, adding, when I failed to jump up, 'Quickly...please!'

My immediate thought was that something had happened to Jamie. In my imagination I pictured his sports car crumpled against a tree on some quiet country road, Jamie slumped against the shattered windscreen, blood dribbling from his mouth, and Louise, dead but completely unmarked, or perhaps just unmarked, sprawled beside him. Gazing distractedly round the room, Mrs Wilkinson said, more to herself than me, 'Where's Jamie? It's hours since he took that girl to the station.'

There were lights on everywhere, but when I got downstairs there was no sign of Mrs Wilkinson, nor any answer when I called her name. Finally I found her in the cloakroom beside the front door, crouched over her husband who lay face down on the red tiled floor, between the lavatory and the door. By the way she was shaking him and shouting, I assumed he must be dead. As I looked on, wondering what to do, I found my attention riveted by details: light falling on the folds in his clothes, the way the torso and legs were twisted, the bluish tint to his face and fingernails. Over the years I've done a lot of life drawing, but until then I hadn't realised how contrived are even the best studio poses; or, conversely, how unnatural and unexpected Mr Wilkinson looked. The nearest I'd been to a dead body was as a child, when I'd gone into a neighbour's garden to fetch a ball and seen through some French windows a corpse laid out on a table. Then I had been mystified, now I felt helpless. In my alarm, my mind reached back to first-aid classes at school when I'd been interested only in making wounds look realistic with lipstick and bits of plasticene.

In the confined space of the cloakroom it was difficult to move Mr Wilkinson, and it took us some time to turn him over. His face was now very pale, and there was a scratch on his temple, but though unconscious, he was still breathing.

Then, while I was in the dining-room, pouring Mrs Wilkinson a drink, I heard a siren and within moments the house was full of people. But my mood was soon transformed from worry – what if Jamie heard what had happened on the radio, what if this, what if that – to fury at his absence. In a flash I saw him for what he was: selfish, manipulative, careless, cold. Where only minutes before I'd imagined him dead against a tree, I now saw him in a cosy clinch, sweet-talking that blond bitch into bed. It was Jamie's fault. I had no doubt of that. But the angrier I became, the more I blamed myself. Was it possible that it had taken me so long to see my friend's real character, or that it should have taken such an event to open my eyes?

Mrs Wilkinson and I stood aside while the ambulance men went to work, lifting her husband out of the cloak-room and onto a stretcher, attaching a drip to his arm, alerting intensive care to expect an emergency. Evidently, he had suffered a serious heart attack but, though unconscious, was not thought to be in any immediate danger; no more would be known until tests had been done. Mrs Wilkinson was very subdued throughout and hardly seemed to notice when she was being spoken to, but when I offered to drive her to the hospital she asked me to wait behind for Jamie and, though it was not something I looked forward to, I could hardly refuse.

In the hours Jamie kept me waiting I rehearsed a brief statement, but when he finally breezed in, pleased as Punch, and began to rattle off some story about his car breaking down, I wanted to throttle him, to shake sense into him in much the same way his mother had been trying to put the life back into her husband.

'Where the hell's everyone? I'm ravenous,' he said, wandering into the kitchen while I trailed behind.

I don't know why it took so long to explain what had happened. Perhaps I was waiting for a suitable moment when there is no such thing, only occasions when one is momentarily less inhibited, or simply no longer able to contain oneself. In the end his restlessness got to me, and in a surprisingly loud voice I heard myself ordering him to sit down and listen.

While I made my little speech, Jamie sat silently, staring at the kitchen table, but as soon as I'd finished he stood up and without speaking rushed from the room. I heard the front door slam and the sound of a car. Then he was back. 'Look,' he said, 'I don't have to tell you, but if anyone calls, you don't know anything.'

'Just go, will you?' I said.

'Good man,' he said, flashing his most insincere smile. 'Make yourself at home. And remember: Mum's the word.' On his way out he promised he would call from the hospital, but he never did. Nor did I expect it. As he might have said, it was just good manners, it didn't mean anything.

Rattling around that big gloomy house, scared

of every creak and shadow, rummaging through bookshelves and family scrapbooks or fidgeting with the remote control television, I longed to be elsewhere. Instead hour after hour I sat staring at the screen, praying that someone would relieve my vigil and that the phone wouldn't ring. Finally, at two o'clock, when no one had returned and I had still heard nothing from Jamie or his mother, I switched off the lights and went up to bed.

I was woken in the morning by what sounded like a bell, but when I reached the front door there was no one there. Unwashed and half asleep, I wandered into the dining-room in search of a cigarette, to find Duncan colonising the dining-table with newspapers and discarded crockery. He looked so much at home I wanted to hit him.

'There's no one here,' he announced. 'I'm holding the fort.'

'Against whom?'

'I wasn't expecting anyone,' he said.

Instead of feeling grateful I found his presence disconcerting. Knowing Duncan, he had dropped in on the off-chance of some free hospitality and knew nothing of what had taken place the night before, but I didn't see why I should be the one to break the news about Mr Wilkinson. He could find that out for himself. So, forgoing breakfast, I went upstairs, packed my things and scribbled a note to Mrs Wilkinson. Suddenly I couldn't get out of that house fast enough. I wanted to be back in London – filthy, noisy, over-crowded London – in my own home and with Janet.

Part Two

1

The Auberge stood on a busy, scrub-lined road on the outskirts of Calais: a nondescript, whitewashed building with brown-painted shutters, tubs of bright flowers and a faded sign in Gothic script. Inside, the walls were paper-thin, the beds wide enough for one person, but that hardly mattered as we had to leave first thing in the morning to be back in London in time for Mr Wilkinson's memorial service.

I don't know how the French do it. Take the hotel's dining-room. It had phoney olde-worlde beams, bulbous brown furniture, brass carriage lamps, checked table-cloths, plastic trolleys, a Chinese lacquer screen, polished horse brasses, an open fireplace and a framed portrait of our beloved Queen behind the bar. Now that, as Bob Rosen might have said, was a room with an identity crisis. It didn't know which country, let alone which century it was living in. But it worked. It was effective. Conspicuous contempt for good taste even made it attractive: in England old buildings are regularly ruined by over-zealous attempts at 'authenticity', and transformed into places in which no one dares raise his voice, let alone his glass.

Not that I'm enamoured of the French – how many Englishmen are? Their refusal to take us seriously is infuriating. But at least they aren't obsessed with class and manners and where the hell you went to school. If the English weren't so stuck-up they might even learn a thing or two about enjoying life. I certainly feel alive the moment my feet touch French soil. Life there seems to be lived with the volume full on. But perhaps one has to be Jewish to appreciate that.

Not that there'd recently been any shortage of volume at home. Since the beginning of the Falklands business one could hardly hear oneself think. The last time I could remember anything like it was as long ago as 1966 when we'd won the World Cup.

By the time we'd left England in the week after Easter I was heartily sick of the Falklands. It didn't take any time to rehearse the arguments pro and con, and my involvement with events seemed to be getting everyone down. My parents, whose apocalyptic view of things is second only to Nostradamus (another Jew, who had consorted with the Goyim!), were mystified by my jingoism. The only time I'd seen my father since the business blew up he'd treated me as if I'd gone mad – not, as he usually does, because I've chosen not to have what he calls a 'proper job', or because I make what he refers to – can you beat it? – as 'graven images', or even because I live with a 'shiksa' and make friends with 'Goyim' – neither of which he could ever trust himself or anyone else enough to do – but simply because he couldn't fathom how I could get worked up about something which was, he insisted, none of my damn business. Despite having been welcomed as a refugee from the Nazis, my father has never thought of England as home, or himself as English, and behaves as though Jewish suffering is somehow different from other people's; as if Jewish blood was a different colour or consistency. He can't see that nowadays we inhabit a multiracial melting-pot in which Jews are no longer singled out for special treatment: that, miracle of miracles, there are actually other people worse off than us. An uncritical supporter of Begin and his bible-thumpers, my father seemed incapable of taking seriously anything that wasn't carved in stone or had been uttered in the last five-thousand years. In such circumstances my mother, usually the peacemaker, was wise to keep her own counsel. She, after all, had to live with him.

For different reasons, Janet was just as sick of hearing me go on about the justice of the British case. The whole enterprise was ridiculous, she insisted; if there had to be a war, we should thank our lucky stars it was far away. What was to me a perfectly legitimate concern with events in the outside world she saw only as an evasion of responsibility, distracting me from important domestic considerations, like getting married, starting a family and God knows what else.

On the Friday after Easter we crossed the Channel to Calais and by nightfall were in Chartres, dining in the shadow of the cathedral. Late the following afternoon, after a long, hot drive, we were knocking back the duty-free in a cottage outside Bordeaux. Our room opened directly onto a vineyard and the air was filled with country smells and the whine of mopeds. From such a vantage it was soon easy to forget events at home, and I began to feel like someone waking fuzzy-headed after a party who wonders if he has made a terrible fool of himself.

A friend in the wine business had commissioned some drawings for a calendar, and in the warm spring sunshine I was soon at work. He had left the choice of subject to me – foolishly perhaps, as there were so many *châteaux* around Bordeaux, and each place we visited was more inviting than the last.

Jamie, no doubt, would have advised me where to go, but for once I was glad he wasn't around. His preoccupation with wine, amusing at first, had finally irritated me over lunch at his club. It spoke of an unaccustomed seriousness, of a friend I no longer knew, of efforts to turn himself into someone he wasn't, of the influence of others. His recent behaviour had been erratic, to say the least. And I was fed up with defending him when it seemed obvious he was only too happy to cast me as a villain. Still, if by going away I hoped to escape further disillusion I needn't have bothered. As we toured the wine country, visiting the museum at Mouton Rothschild, or lingered over lunch on a terrace in St Emilion, or when, late in the afternoon, we sipped young wines in failing sunlight at dusty roadsides, my mood was elegiac; and even Janet, who after five years should have been used to my moods, couldn't fail to notice the extent of my self-absorption.

It was in Bordeaux that I read of Mr Wilkinson's death. Janet had been teasing me for behaving like a 'typical Englishman' abroad, and to refute this imputation I tried to see how long I could survive without an English newspaper. I cheated, of course, slipping out to the car to listen to the World Service news, but otherwise surprised myself by my ability to do without. Events in the South Atlantic were hotting up. The runway at Port Stanley had already been bombed: attacks on the fleet were expected any time; the peace process, such as it was, had – to my relief – collapsed. But with Mr Wilkinson's death that all seemed secondary and suddenly remote.

What he would have made of recent events was anyone's guess. At that ghastly last supper the Falklands hadn't been so much as mentioned, but one could be sure he'd have had something interesting and unexpected to say. A strong opponent of unilateralism, he was out of step with mainstream party opinion, but as a young lawyer at the end of the war he'd been involved in the Nuremberg trials and knew that evil must be met with any weapons to hand. A good listener, always more interested in what you had to say than in his own opinion, he had lacked the ruthlessness and singlemindedness, the hunger and vanity, characteristic of most politicians, and would probably have agreed with the obituarist who suggested that his gregariousness was to blame for his failure to fulfil people's expectations of him. Beholden to no one, he had nevertheless been liked by almost everyone.

Whether the same would ever be said about Jamie remained to be seen. Though he had more than his share of vanity, I admired the way he avoided, without ever appearing rebellious or bloody-minded, trying to step into his father's shoes. No doubt he had any number of clever and convincing arguments to justify his recent change of heart: that he'd always been interested in politics; that he'd been biding his time; that his views were his own; that it was no one else's concern. He might have added that politics was in a sense his family business. One thing not even Jamie would have had the gall to claim was that he had a lot to offer people. In friendship – as in love – I had long ago accepted that he was a taker, not a giver.

The dining-room was crowded when we came downstairs, so we waited at the bar for a table. Nearby, a group of middle-aged, middle-class Englishmen were celebrating something or other. Like us, they had missed the last ferry – I'd seen one of them haranguing an impassive official at the ferry-terminal – but I'd no wish to be identified with them. With their booming voices and offhand manners they seemed to think they owned the place.

'Must you?' Janet said, as I went on about them. 'They're only enjoying themselves.'

'I can't stand the way they assume everyone is interested in them. It's so English ... If Jamie were here he'd put them in their place.'

'Thank God he isn't! For a fortnight you haven't stopped telling me what a nightmare he is, but the moment anyone agrees with you, you jump to his defence. At least be consistent.'

'Why? Slagging off one's friends is one of the privileges of friendship.'

'Not all the time.'

'How did we get on to this anyway?' I said, trying to change the subject.

'If you really want to know, you were sitting there like a stuck pig pretending to not be English and not fooling anyone for a second.'

'I wasn't pretending,' I said. 'I'm proud of it.'

'Course you are, old man. Quite right too. Have a drink. *Un boisson pour mon vieux ami ici. Pardon, deux boissons...*'

While we'd been talking one of the boorish

expats had sneaked up and was offering to buy us a drink. I pretended he wasn't there, but Janet, who's always more interested than I am in meeting new people, immediately struck up a conversation about God knows what, so I left them to it.

Of course, Janet was only doing it to annoy me. She never could accept my ambivalence towards Jamie, because she had this mad idea that I really wanted to be like him. Women don't respond to reason, least of all her, and the last thing she'd ever admit to was jealousy – though why on earth she should have felt jealous of Jamie was beyond me.

When their conversation had gone on long enough I muttered something in her ear.

Immediately, the man said: 'Why don't you two lovebirds stop arguing and have another drink – in celebration.'

'What's there to celebrate?'

'Where've you been, old boy? Bloody marvellous news. Our chaps have sunk an Argie battleship.' He began making noises in impersonation of an explosion, sending saliva and gin all over us. 'That'll teach the bastards to invade sovereign British territory,' he added, unfurling a handkerchief from his breast pocket, which I half expected to be coloured red, white and blue.

I raised my eyebrows at Janet, who began to giggle, and asked, 'When?'

'Today. Yesterday. What's it matter? Point is, we've given the dago a bloody nose. Next time he'll think twice ... *Monsieur!*'

Then one of his friends called to him, and after kissing Janet's hand he returned unsteadily to his table.

Smiling, Janet said: 'I wish we didn't have to rush back. We're having such a good time and you know what it'll be like.'

'He's my best friend. I owe his family everything.'

'It's always Jamie this, Jamie that. Can't you live without him for five minutes?'

'You're tired,' I said. ' You haven't eaten all day. I'm going to see about our table,' But it was only to escape her criticism that I left my seat. Once started on the subject of Jamie, she was like a dog with a bone. As I sat down again, she said: 'Christ, if I didn't know better, I'd think you fancied him.'

'You know blonds aren't my type.'

'But I'm blonde.'

'Quite!'

'If Jamie's really such a great friend why's he always trying to get me into bed?'

'It's nothing personal. He does it to everyone.'

'Even so, I wish he'd stop calling me at work.'

'Anyway what if he *does* fancy you?' I said. 'Sometimes even I do. He's going through a bad patch, that's all. His father's just died, for Christ's sake.'

At last relief arrived, and we were shown to a table in a quiet corner of the room. But in the long, awkward silences which punctuated the meal, there were moments when I stared enviously at the boor and his cronies whooping it up, moments when I'd far rather have been with them than with Janet, toasting 'The Queen' and 'Death to the Dago'.

2

That Gerald Wilkinson had been greatly loved
must have been obvious to everyone at his
packed memorial service. Though not a house-
hold name, even my father grudgingly admitted
to having listened to him briefly on *Any Questions*:
a decent, easy-going, middle-of-the-road Labour
back-bencher, who was as frank and engaging
answering non-political questions as he was
transparently ill-at-ease defending the latest
lunatic Party Conference decision or specimen of
trade union bloody-mindedness.

There were those on the left of the party who
insinuated that he'd be more at home quaffing
claret with Roy Jenkins and the other bourgeois
revisionists in the newly-formed Social Democra-
tic Party: people who saw Gerald Wilkinson as
emblematic of all that conciliation, warm-
heartedness, even temper, generosity of spirit,
ideological flabbiness and sentimentality had
failed to bring about in modern Britain: the
Fabian and Trustee of Dartington Hall who
might have ended up on the crossbenches in the

House of Lords, rather than the hardworking member of Amnesty International and other Civil Rights organisations trouble-shooting the world at his own expense in support of free speech.

The company at the Wilkinsons' had always been remarkable for its variety. One was as likely to find oneself talking to some liberationist African bishop, resplendent in shocking pink, as some moody musician from behind the Iron Curtain or loud-mouthed refugee from Macarthyism; and though Mr Wilkinson had been only sixty at his death it was hard to imagine him feeling many regrets. Life had been good to him, and he'd been good to a great many people, and if, as some newspapers had suggested, he'd spread himself thinly he'd been none the less impressive for it.

The service, when finally it got started, was brief and non-denominational: an Old Testament psalm, the hymn 'Jerusalem', a favourite Shakespeare sonnet, followed by a few words from an ex-Prime Minister, little of which I could hear. Then there was a prayer from no particular religion, a burst of Bach on the organ, and before I knew it I was outside again, buffeted by fleeing figures, their collars turned up against the wind. In my mind I was searching for Jamie, but when the crowds cleared I found Bob instead, taking a nip from a hip flask. His blotchy face was covered with bits of tissue and his hands shook as he tried to light a cigarette.

I said: 'Why's everyone in such a hurry?'

'Haven't you heard? The Argies have sunk the

Sheffield ... About bloody time!'

'Christ! When?'

'Yesterday. Where've you been?'

'I only got back from France this morning. I haven't seen a paper.'

He took another drink, lit a cigarette from one he was already smoking and proffered his flask.

'Thanks, but I'll wait,' I said. Then I changed my mind and took a long swig. As I felt my face flush deeply in the crisp air I thought of those loud-mouths in Calais, whose boorishness had made me feel ashamed of being English but whose cameraderie I'd found enviable. They wouldn't be smiling now, I thought, without pleasure.

'Makes a great picture,' Robert said, producing a newspaper from his coat. 'Beats Capa any day.'

'That one of the *Belgrano* really hit me,' I said.

'Not as hard as it hit the *Belgrano*, old boy!'

'Very funny,' I said. 'As for that headline in the *Sun*, I never thought Fleet Street could sink that low.'

'Don't underestimate us. It perfectly summed up the mood of the country in its finest hour!'

When I failed to say anything he added: 'It was bound to happen sooner or later. You knew that. At least now not so many people think it's just a bloody lark.'

'Not me,' I said, but I knew what he was driving at. For weeks now, a lot of people had been carrying on as if war was just a game: a simple way of solving inconvenient problems. I'd

97

never met an Argentinian in my life, but I had no illusions about that country's government. Galtieri, Costa Mendes, Anaya and anyone associated with that brutal comic-opera regime didn't give a damn about human life, Argentinian or British. Even so, photographs of the destruction of HMS *Sheffield* left me surprisingly cold. I had grown up on a diet of Second World War films – *Sink the Bismarck*, *The Battle of the River Plate*, *In Which We Serve* – grim, grey pictures of naval life in which Jack Hawkins was forever on the bridge peering at the horizon through binoculars and Sam Kydd cracking jokes down below; the sea, like the Germans themselves, cold and merciless. In the end they always went down, and we limped home, bruised but victorious.

Unlike the sinking of the *Belgrano*, the destruction of HMS *Sheffield* was something out of *Star Wars*, a spectacular fireworks display which seemed unconnected with real life. And although it was impossible not to know that behind the fireworks people were dying horribly I was far less affected by it than by the picture of the *Belgrano* slipping beneath the waves. Younger people would, I know, feel differently. All the same, my equivocal reaction to these two disasters surprised me more than I had ever imagined I would by anything that happened in that remote corner of the world.

I'd have liked to express at least some of this to Bob. If not to my oldest friend, to whom could I speak of such things? To Janet, who took no interest in what was going on? To my father, who cared only about wars involving Israel? To Jamie, who was interested in the war's outcome only in so far as it affected his political prospects? Regrettably, Bob had long ago written me off as yet another knee-jerk Imperialist who believed that recovering the Falklands was an honourable endeavour, and I had no desire to be mocked by his condescension.

As it happened, just at that moment Jamie and his mother appeared on the church steps, and after an affectionate exchange and an invitation to lunch I turned to tell Bob that I wouldn't be joining him in the pub, but by then he had disappeared.

When I arrived at Jamie's flat, the front door was standing open and a man in a white jacket was taking charge of coats. Noise came from a room at the top of the stairs, but when I walked in I was momentarily convinced that I was at the wrong address. An effort had been made to remove the customary impression of a place left in a hurry – the sports gear and Japanese woodcuts, London Library books and bunch of tarnished trophies had in all probability been slung into a cupboard, to resurface as soon as the reception was over, as I hoped my friend's old personality would also. What made me think I wasn't in the right place were the pictures: vast, unframed, abstract canvasses, leaning up against every wall, which were so without merit that I knew I wouldn't be able to restrain myself.

Jamie was at the far end of the long reception-room behind a table laid out with glasses and bottles. I was dying to ask about the pictures, but he looked busy and it didn't seem appropriate, and when finally I brought them up he refused to look at me, indicating by a sudden flurry of activity that he had no time for small-talk. But when I failed to follow up my enquiry he said, rather too casually: 'Oh, the pics? They're Lou's. Cheer the place up a bit, don't they?'

While in the process of opening a bottle, he glanced surreptitiously at the walls. Perhaps he wanted my approval. Painting was, after all, one subject I knew something about. When I again didn't respond, he added: 'You met her briefly. At Easter.'

'The stone-faced blonde who gave you a dose?'

'For God's sake, keep your voice down.'

'You got it seen to, I hope?'

'It was nothing. Psoriasis. I probably caught it from a towel.'

'Isn't that a nervous condition?' I asked.

'Well, anyway, it's gone. Thank God,' he said, wandering off with a tray. I remained where I was, and in a couple of minutes he was back. As if there'd been no interruption he said: 'You know, at first I wasn't sure about them, whether they fitted in. They're a bit overpowering, I'll admit. Now they've been here a while I'm beginning to like them. Frankly, the old place needed a change.'

'Like the Jews needed Hitler!' Then something occurred to me, and I said: 'You don't mean Louise painted them?'

'What did you think?'

'On her own? Without help?'

'I suppose so. Why?'

'No reason.'

'Well, anyway,' he said, 'I like them. The way they're just propped against the walls ... more like objects really.'

'In the round? You mean like sculpture?' I said.

'Yes. Something like that.' Then he looked up and saw I was grinning and said: 'For God's sake! She's only nineteen. She needs a leg up.'

'You mean a leg-over!'

Unexpectedly touched by this display of loyalty, I then said: 'What does Jennifer make of them?'

'Haven't you heard? We've split up.'

'Not because of the pictures, surely?'

'Very funny.'

'You mean she finally decided she'd had enough.'

'It didn't seem to be going anywhere, that's all.'

I knew exactly what he meant. At times I felt the same about Janet. I said: 'So Lou's moved in?'

'Not exactly. She shares a flat near her art school. Living in two places would be too complicated. For the time being, anyway.'

'She's at art school?'

'Give it a rest, will you?'

'If I'd known she was at art school I'd have given her a few tips. As the moyl said to the actress!'

'Things were a bit tricky at Easter. You might have fancied her. Or worse, she might have fancied you.'

'I'm flattered', I said, 'but she was your guest.'

'Come off it!' he said.

'When you shit on your own doorstep, you usually end up sleeping on it. Of course, if she'd been with Duncan ...'

'Well, anyway,' he said. 'I'm no longer worried on that score.'

'Glad to hear it,' I said, suddenly and unexpectedly jealous. 'When you've been around students as long as I have you begin to crave someone your own age.'

Jamie went off again while I sniffed around the flat like an insurance man investigating a dubious claim. There were no more than thirty people, mostly at the other end of the room, but I didn't feel like mingling – at least not until I found myself standing next to Duncan, who was trying to listen in on half-a-dozen conversations simultaneously without drawing attention to himself. Encouraged by the evident discomfort my presence gave him, I said, 'Missed the boat, have we? Shouldn't you be in the South Seas by now, serenading our glorious fighting men with *Bali Hi*?' Duncan sang in a choir somewhere and for all I knew had a good voice, but the urge to deflate him was always irresistible. Nevertheless, it was a pretty lame effort and I was glad Jamie was out of earshot.

'I've seen you since then,' he said.

For the moment I'd forgotten finding him at breakfast the morning after Mr Wilkinson's heart-attack and said: 'If you're still here, who's keeping an eye on the chaps at the front ... or perhaps you don't care?'

'I care as much as the next man. The next Englishman, anyway,' he added, avoiding my gaze. Then, refilling his glass, he added: 'Just typical! There are always cynics ready to scoff when British soldiers' lives are put at risk.'

It had been a poor effort on my part, but I didn't deserve this. 'Since when were you on the *Sun*?' I said. 'You've worn out more pairs of trousers sitting on the fence than anyone I know.' I refilled my glass and smiled inwardly. If only Jamie could have heard that, I thought.

'I wouldn't expect you to understand', Duncan said, taking a step back. 'But suppose there's another crisis in the Middle East, a steep rise in oil prices, something involving vital national interests?'

'We have our own oil. We're no longer dependent on the Arabs ... thank God.'

'I was speaking hypothetically,' Duncan said.

'People like you always do.'

'Look at America. Anyone can see how time and again its best interests are perverted by the Jewish lobby.'

'Where I came from it's called a foyer,' I said.

'So you think Jews aren't loyal, is that it?'

'You said it, not me.'

'But it's what you meant,' I said. 'Anyway this isn't the States, and you exaggerate our importance. We're only one of any number of special interest groups looking after their own, when no one else will.'

'Even more reason.'

I had nothing further to say to him, nothing to offer in argument that he couldn't bend to his purposes. Until that moment I hadn't realised how powerless Duncan must have felt. But I didn't feel sorry for him.

'I suppose you think these atrocious daubs are Art with a capital A,' I said, changing the subject. 'Christ, if I thought Jamie would still speak to me I'd come back with a tin of primer and scrub the whole lot out. There's more than five hundred square feet of canvas here going begging. You've no idea how many classes I have to teach to afford that. In the long run he'd thank me.'

'If you ask me, they're a distinct improvement,' he said. 'They show he's growing up at last. Those cosy water-colours were far too sentimental. As for those prints, I'm glad Jamie at least had the decency to hide them away.'

'They were too direct for you, I expect,' I said.

'Obvious perhaps.'

'Have it your own way,' I said.

'I never thought I'd say this,' Duncan went on, 'but purchasing these works of art represents a new departure for Jamie. The undergraduate phase of his life is over. And not before time, if I may say so.'

'He paid for them?'

'She doesn't look the kind of girl who'd give anything away.'

'No, I suppose not,' I said. 'And what phase of life do you think he's passed into?' Although I put this question with a straight face, I hardly expected him to take me seriously.

'Haven't you heard?' he said.

'What?'

'He's standing for Parliament. At least, that's his intention.'

I glared at Duncan. Suddenly I didn't like the direction in which the conversation was going. 'Who persuaded him?' I asked.

'His friends. Those of us who care about his future.'

'How could you? We all know Labour's desperate, but Jamie ...'

'Seriously, you didn't know? In three weeks his name goes before the selection committee. Amazingly he's already got a union to nominate him.'

Duncan then mentioned the name of the constituency and everything fell into place.

'But that's his father's,' I said. 'He can't be serious?'

'There's going to be a General Election in the next couple of years, and it may be a lot sooner. If things go wrong in the Falklands, even under Michael Foot Labour can hardly fail to get in.

Either way, now's the perfect time to blood Jamie.'

'That's easy to say when it isn't your blood.'

'Just a figure of speech.'

'Tell that to the crew of HMS *Sheffield*,' I said.

'They were professionals. They knew what they were in for.'

'They hadn't any choice, and you know it,' I said. 'No doubt you also expect Jamie to lose the by-election?'

'Between you and me, he hasn't a hope of being adopted. Militants have sewn the place up, lock stock and barrel. Anyway, Labour's never gone in for dynastic stuff. He should know that.'

'I thought he'd already been nominated?'

'Nominated, not adopted. By a union, not by the Party.'

'I see,' I said, though I didn't. 'And how much of this does Jamie know?'

'How should I know?'

'You must have some idea.'

'Put it this way. If he doesn't, he's no business going into politics.'

'Quite!' I said, and walked away.

I didn't stay much longer. Jamie was tied up looking after the guests, and apart from the Wilkinsons themselves I hardly knew a soul.

Irritable and depressed, I felt like putting my feet up somewhere quiet, well away from other people. But I still had some chores to do that afternoon, and it was dark before I got home.

It had been an important day for a great many

people. The sight of all those politicians hurrying from the service was a poignant reminder, if any were needed, that the business of recapturing the Falklands had hardly begun; also, that there was political capital still to be made out of British reversals. Voices which had gone quiet would now be shouting for a negotiated end to a collective madness which had found perfect expression in the *Sun*'s massive headline, celebrating the sinking of the *Belgrano*: GOTCHA!

In spite of all I'd learned since the beginning of the crisis I accepted the justice of the British case. Over the years successive British governments had undoubtedly sent conflicting signals to Argentina, but it was now too late to back down. Whatever else one might say about the Prime Minister – that she was insensitive, pig-headed and never listened, that she had little understanding of history or of Britain's true place in the world – backing down was not her way. Any hesitation, moreover, would only encourage those murderous bastards in Buenos Aires. What, after all, would the families of the dead and wounded think, if we pulled out now? I wouldn't have liked to be in their shoes; nor, for that matter, in the Prime Minister's. But after the attack on HMS *Sheffield*, my fingers were more firmly crossed than ever. One missile had destroyed a million illusions: now was a time for silent prayer, not angry voices or banner headlines. As Jamie had been saying from the very beginning, it was too late in the day for gunboat diplomacy, but it was also no time to turn back.

While listening to the News I sorted through the mail. There were some gallery invitations, a postcard from someone I hadn't seen in years and to my surprise, for I couldn't remember her ever writing to me before, a note from Jamie's mother asking me to lunch.

I poured myself a drink and wondered what she could possibly want, and was still trying to work it out when Janet walked in.

'Guess where I've been?' she said, hanging up her coat.

'I give up.'

'At least try.'

'I'm not in the mood,' I said.

'Even if it concerns your precious friend Jamie?'

'Go on,' I said.

'Jennifer rang just after I got in. I could tell it was you she really wanted. She was in a bit of a state.'

'That's hardly surprising,' I said.

'She's at her wits' end. She doesn't know what to do.'

'I'm sorry it's that bad. I've always liked her,' I said. To my astonishment Janet then burst out laughing.

'Trust you to get the wrong end of the stick,' she said, pecking me on the cheek. 'Jennifer's fine. It's your chum who's cracking up.'

'Really? He seemed in one piece a couple of hours ago.'

'I'm only repeating what she said.'

'Quite.'

'Evidently he's taken to mooning about outside her flat at all hours. She opens the curtains in the morning and he's standing there looking hangdog, and when she gets home in the evening he's still waiting. You'd think he'd have better things to do.'

'No one likes to admit they've been given the boot,' I said.

'I'm amazed it took her so long to see the light, but she was always a bit dim. It seems to have come as quite a blow to old macho man's self-esteem.'

'He'll recover,' I said.

'Serves the bastard right, if you ask me.'

'What's it to you?' I said. 'She's been going out with him for God knows how long. She knew the score.'

'Love is blind...and all that.'

'Jennifer's hardly Helen Keller!'

'You know what some women are like,' Janet said. 'They love going into every detail about their lovers.'

'And?' I said, thinking that if this were true they were quite unlike men in that respect.

'You know how over-sexed Jamie is. Well, one day he suddenly stopped wanting to sleep with her. He didn't even want to be in the same bed. But he wouldn't give any reason, and when she asked him he just blew up. As it happened, she was due for a check-up, and it turned out she'd caught something. Gonorrhoea, I think. She realised immediately that Jamie must have given it to her. Of course he denied it. Trust him! If he'd only come clean she wouldn't have minded.'

'Fat chance,' I said.

'Not only that. He then started to blame her, insisting she must have caught it from someone else. Apparently he got quite hysterical and accused her of everything under the sun. She thinks it's to do with his father dying. She said he'd never been like that before and it really frightened her. He'd always been so controlled.'

'That's hardly a reason to split up', I said. 'Not after all that time.'

'She thought it would all blow over too, until she heard that he was going round with some schoolgirl.'

'Lou's a bit older than that,' I said.

'You mean you knew all along?'

'No, not exactly.'

'Well, anyway', Janet said, 'she thought you might be able to help. You know, a friendly word in his ear.'

'You know what he's like when his mind's made up,' I said. 'She'd do better to work on Duncan, though it was probably him who blew the whistle in the first place.'

For some reason this seemed to annoy Janet, who said: 'You're always so rude about him. What harm's he ever done you?'

'He's a shit-stirrer. He loves to make trouble.'

'Then why do you spend so much time together?'

'Oh, I don't know. Perhaps I find him irresistible! Anyway, why does it matter? He and Jamie are inseparable. Good enough?'

'If you say so.'

'From the way he goes on you'd think Duncan was in love with him or something.'

Janet suddenly looked up and gave me a long, hard stare. After a few moments I began to feel quite uncomfortable and said: 'Did I say something?'

'Maybe. I don't know.' Then she looked away again and said: 'Duncan's always been perfectly nice to me.'

'To your face, perhaps.' I was by now bored with the whole subject and said: 'You know, Jennifer's probably better off without him. It's not as if Jamie's about to change his spots.' I began to chuckle. 'Spots – Gonorrhoea. Get it?'

'You haven't been listening, as usual. She can't get rid of him.'

'Same difference,' I said.

'Hardly! Still, perhaps he'll stop pestering her once he finds out his behaviour's common knowledge.'

'Tell him yourself if you feel that strongly.'

'He'd never listen. Not to a woman, anyway.'

Can you blame him? I thought, but said nothing.

3

Mrs Wilkinson had written that she hoped we could meet very soon, but once the art school reopened I didn't have a moment to myself. There were projects to plan and timetables to organise, and as usual no one knew where they should be or when. Students who'd chosen their courses months before were suddenly desperate to change departments, and in the midst of it all the Principal suddenly announced his retirement. As in any small, enclosed world we have our share of time-servers and slackers, troublemakers, *prima donnas*, neurotics, hypochondriacs and over-sexed Jack-the-Lads, and the last thing anyone needed was that kind of upheaval. Most of the staff are only professional artists trying to subsidise their own work. Inevitably some end up teaching full time, and the school couldn't do without them – they're usually the most dependable, willing to take over classes at short notice or perform the dull chores – but in general any more than three days teaching a week is discouraged, and with good reason.

One particular teacher is to be found in the pub at the beginning of every term, surrounded by nubile foundation students, prattling on about how he doesn't believe in teaching art at all, but he comes back every year and, though he'd never admit it, is excellent at the job. Despite conflicting opinions on almost everything, we all rub along pretty well, only taking care not to break one cardinal rule: never interfere with another teacher's project if you find yourself taking his class. Students at least have a right to know what's expected, especially as most of them would rather do anything than sit drawing for hours on a hard wooden donkey in an overcrowded studio, just as most of the staff would also prefer to be doing something else, usually with one of the students.

As a teacher I've no illusions about myself. I haven't the patience to be any good. In the Life Room it's easy to be lazy. Most people have no idea how to look because they've never learnt how to forget what they know, and it takes time and patience to get someone back to that state of innocence where nothing has a name or a definite shape.

Despite all my grumbles, I love the school and would probably go mad without the human contact it provides – which after five years in the job is the only reason I'm prepared to get up at the crack of dawn three mornings a week and *schlep* halfway across London, to make sure that little Lord Tarquin with the vermilion Mohican haircut, or baby Francesca from Kensington with the ring through her nose and size eleven Doc Marten's doesn't skive off immediately after signing the register.

On the morning of my lunch with Mrs Wilkinson I took the first-year painters to a show at the Whitechapel Gallery, after which I left them to their own devices. I couldn't make them into artists – only they could do that – and whether producing sketches or finished drawings, or jotting down ideas for future projects, they were expected to use their time productively. One or two of them showed real promise, and I was curious to see what they made of Spitalfields and Petticoat Lane, places worlds away from the quiet, leafy streets and stately stucco houses in which many of them had grown up. But it's often the most gifted who fail to come on – talent, like charm, being an attribute of little use without anything to back it up – and if they chose to spend all day playing pool or thinking of what to wear in the evening I couldn't prevent it.

After arranging to meet up late in the afternoon I had an hour to kill, and without really thinking where I was going I set off on foot in the direction of Commercial Road.

It was almost twenty years since I'd accompanied my father on his Sunday morning sorties to the East End. It was a mystery why he'd insisted on going all that way to buy gefilte fish, smoked salmon and salt beef when there were perfectly good delicatessens in North London. It wasn't as though he'd grown up there and felt nostalgic. Perhaps he thought it was good for the car – he was the quintessential Sunday driver – or the slums reminded him in some way of the 'old country', as he referred to it, though God knows it didn't sound as if there was anything worth remembering there. As is often the case, he probably didn't know the answer himself but, having started something, it soon became part of his inviolable routine. I only went along to make sure we were back in time for lunch, but I still remembered the enormous man behind the counter who slipped me slivers of smoked salmon while the old man's back was turned, and the envy I felt when some spoilt little kid with a rich American dad was given the run of the place.

Apart from a few *schmutter* shops with exotic names hardly any Jews remained there, but as if in a dream I was struck every few steps by the juxtaposition of the familiar and strange, of the old peeking out from behind the new, which made me wonder whether I'd been there before or was only trying to will something into being.

Wandering back and forth down the narrow, ragged streets I soon lost track of time, and when I looked at my watch I realised I was going to be late for lunch. Anxiously retracing my steps, I turned a corner and found myself in front of the old delicatessen, and before I knew it I was standing inside on the slippery stone floor, taking in the rows and rows of rusty biscuit tins and dusty jars, the wooden pickle barrels and trays of fishballs; the tubs of chopped liver and chopped herring, the fatty slab of salt beef steaming on its wooden board, and the necklaces of Viennas; voluptuous watermelons, cheeses, pastries, boxes of matzos, strudels, cheesecakes and jars of purple borscht.

Somewhere behind the counter a voice asked me to hang on, and in a moment I found myself facing the man from my childhood, with his Sumo wrestler's shape, dark moustache and bobbled winter hat, and that same deep, unmistakable voice combining at once, like the best Jewish jokes, helpfulness, impatience, humour and resignation.

'Take your time. Tell me when you're ready. It's what I'm here for,' he said, disappearing again. A moment later his face peered out from between packets of *lockshen* soup.'So don't keep me in suspense. What'll you have? Viennas are very good. The salmon's the best you've ever tasted, take my word. Guaranteed!'

I looked around helplessly, wanting to buy something but quite unable to make up my mind. Squinting at me, he said, 'Don't I know you? Aren't you what's-'is-name's boy? How is the miserable so-and-so? Still giving *tsaurus*, I'll bet!'

'Look,' I said, grinning with pleasure, 'I really have to go. I should be in town by now. But I'll be back, I promise.'

Bored rather than malevolent, this man who

day in, day out for the past forty years had put up with the same indecisiveness, heard and repeated the same jokes, now said without a trace of sentimentality: 'Come whenever you like. Where else am I going to be? Except Saturday, Sundays only till two. If it's bagels you want come early, or even better, phone.' And, turning away, his enormous bulk disappeared again behind a curtain of Frankfurters.

Mrs Wilkinson was waiting for me when I arrived at the restaurant: a small, neat, middle-aged woman, wearing a tailored tweed suit and a sparkling brooch on her lapel, partly hidden behind a menu at the end of a long, narrow room hung with gilt mirrors and fussy parchment wall lamps which resembled an Edwardian railway carriage.

On hearing whom I was meeting, the *maître d'* led me to the table, then flapped about pulling out chairs and unravelling napkins like a conjuror who can't find his rabbit. I'd been greatly looking forward to lunch, but his antics and my lateness only contributed to my discomfort, and when at last he buggered off I made a feeble joke at his expense which went down like a lead balloon.

I don't know why I felt so edgy. Mrs Wilkinson knew how to put people at their ease, and there was nothing in her greeting to suggest that anything between us had changed. Possibly my anxiety had more to do with Jamie. I didn't know

117

why she'd invited me, and I was anticipating some request which would compromise my loyalty to him. But I was also anxious to unburden myself and knew that with little encouragement I might say too much. Though sympathetic and charming, Mrs Wilkinson was not someone I could take into my confidence. Nor could she be expected to welcome some of the things I was likely to say about her son.

Jamie, however, seemed to be the last person on her mind: the reasons for her invitation – 'though one never needs an excuse to see old friends' – to commission a portrait of her late husband. She approached the subject in such a roundabout way that I assumed she was only trying to pick my brains. When at last it dawned on me that this was her way of asking me to do it, I accepted without thinking – an act of impetuosity I was later to regret.

By then we were on to our main course and most of the way through a bottle of Chablis. Relaxed for the first time, I realised just how nervous I'd been feeling and, to make up for lost time, found myself jumping in with both feet.

'It isn't really true Jamie's standing for Parliament?' I asked.

My question, coming out of the blue, seemed to startle her. She wrinkled her nose in a way which recalled Jamie in moments of acute anxiety, then suggested we talk about something else.

'Surely your husband would have been pleased?' I continued, refilling her glass.

118

For a while conversation was interrupted by a fish bone which had lodged in Mrs Wilkinson's throat. I passed her some bread, and by the time a waiter had brought some water the problem was solved.

As if there'd been no interruption, Mrs Wilkinson said, rather fiercely: 'On the contrary. Gerald was always opposed to Jamie pursuing a political career. We both did our best to discourage him.' Then, less forcefully, she added, 'We all knew he was too sensitive for the rough and tumble of politics.'

'I never believed he was that interested.'

'You'd be surprised. He was always trying to help his father, especially when it came to canvassing. Jamie can be very persuasive, you know.'

She seemed to think I was attacking him, which I wasn't, and I said: 'Still, that's not the same as standing oneself, is it?'

I felt a bit like a drunk trying to find a keyhole in the dark, surprising myself and, I suspect, Mrs Wilkinson, more by my frankness than my perspicacity. From time to time she nodded in what I took to be agreement, but when I finally stopped she said, as if she hadn't been listening, 'I can't see why anyone would put himself through such hell if he wasn't serious.'

'Serious about what?'

'About change. About people. What other reason could anyone possibly have?'

'I don't know,' I said.

'Don't underestimate Jamie. He's a dark horse in many ways.'

'I know.'

'It's precisely because he's serious that I worry. To him it's still a game, with rules and conventions. He doesn't realise how ruthless these people can be.'

'The Tories aren't that bad,' I said, stepping onto dangerous ground.

'Not them! It's our Party I'm worried about. I couldn't bear the same to happen to Jamie.'

'But your husband was a great success. He loved the life.'

'If you must know, the last few years have been hell. One long nightmare. Militants made Gerald's life a misery. All our lives, for that matter. Of course, he got no help. Just because show-offs like Tony Benn appear so ridiculous people think they're no threat to anyone. But wait till it happens to them. Of course, the Party's always been a battleground. The Falklands are only a distraction from the important issues. And we're as much to blame. You can't just wait for the other side to make a hash of things. Jamie's right. Thatcher may thoroughly deserve to be out, but we don't deserve to be in again. Not that such things are ever judged on their merits. And of course, Jamie didn't exactly help, egging his father on like that when he knew Gerald had been told to take it easy. He seemed to think his father didn't want to fight when the matter was already out of his hands. As for some of the things he said, Jamie had no cause, not to his father of all people. Gerry was always a fighter.'

'Is that what they were arguing about at Easter?' I asked.

'I don't remember a great deal. It's still rather a blur. But I'm not surprised Jamie's said nothing. He's good reason to feel ashamed. Afterwards he didn't put a foot wrong. He couldn't have been more supportive, but by then it was too late. The damage was done.'

I wanted to know exactly what Jamie had said, but couldn't bring myself to ask. Instead I said, 'He hasn't been himself recently.'

'He seems to think I have influence, but I haven't. None at all. And when he doesn't get adopted he'll feel let down. Of course, he's no longer a child; he must make up his own mind. If I said anything he'd only think I was trying to thwart him, just as he thought his father was. But we were only trying to protect him. The fact is one can't stop people making mistakes. They have to learn the hard way.'

'He seems pleased to have been made a partner in the firm,' I said. 'That's something, isn't it?'

'Oh that!' she said, 'Gerald only arranged it because he thought it might make Jamie act more responsibly. He could've been on the board years ago if he'd taken an interest. But he just went through the motions. It's something he's very good at. There was also some trouble about not turning up for work, but I expect you know about that.'

I nodded, though I hadn't a clue what she was referring to; as I've said, Jamie and I never talked about his work.

'And as if that wasn't enough, he picks that moment to split up with Jennifer. Just when they seemed to be getting on so well, too. I can't think why he did it, but you know as well as I do one can never ask him anything, he just gets furious. He's like his father in that respect. It's an old-fashioned thing to say, but we both hoped they'd settle down and start a family.'

'There's still plenty of time,' I said, thinking of similar questions, only framed in reverse, which I got from my father: 'You're not going to marry that shiksa? When are you going to find yourself a nice Jewish girl? Isn't it about time you started going out with one of your own kind?' Your own kind! I ask you!

'From what I hear he's now going around with someone half his age,' Mrs Wilkinson said. 'Still, it's none of my business.'

'She's an art student,' I said. 'Very pretty. Surely you remember her at Easter?'

But Mrs Wilkinson didn't seem to remember anything much of that weekend, and after this the conversation dried up. For an uncomfortable few minutes I gazed out of the window at all the comings and goings outside Victoria Station, trying to absorb everything I'd learned over lunch. When the waiter had brought our coffee, Mrs Wilkinson leaned across the table and smiled at me.

122

'You know, Dan', she said, 'I've always admired you for the way you manage to support yourself doing something you obviously enjoy. It's a rare gift. You mustn't waste it.'

'I don't intend to,' I said, smiling sweetly.

'I only wish Jamie were as self-reliant as you.'

I'd heard enough about Jamie, and felt like talking about myself. I said, 'I suppose I am lucky. At school I was pretty hopeless, but for some reason I always knew what I wanted to do.'

Actually, I didn't feel all that lucky, but I didn't think she wanted to hear about that. 'You can't blame Jamie,' I added. 'He's got so many talents he's rather spoiled for choice.'

'Oh, Jamie'll be all right,' she said. 'I just don't like the direction he seems to be going in. Of course, it was never easy for him when his father was alive. Politics took up so much of Gerry's time and he could be rather heavy-handed with the children. Sometimes he seemed to forget he wasn't addressing a political meeting. Of course, it didn't help Jamie being the eldest. Simon wasn't nearly as clever, but he was always more contented. I expect Jamie feels he wasn't paid enough attention. It's easier to see these things afterwards. At the time we were all under the influence of Spock. So you see,' she said, as if I wasn't the only one who needed convincing, 'it hasn't been all that easy for him.'

'I'm sure it hasn't,' I muttered, glancing out of the window again and finding it difficult to feel sorry for him. Compared to most people Jamie'd had a pretty cushy time of it. Not that one could blame her for backing him up. In the end you either take friends or leave them; with family, things are never as simple or straightforward.

'Still, I must say,' Mrs Wilkinson said, attracting the waiter's attention, 'I do sometimes wonder if he arrived at this decision entirely on his own.'

'Quite.'

'Of course, in the long run, I don't expect it'll do him any harm. He's bound to learn from the experience and one can hardly blame him for trying. After all, as Gerry always said, it is the best club in London.'

'Jamie will certainly like that,' I said, trying not to smile.

4

'You've heard the news?' my mother asked, as soon as I lifted the receiver.

'Marvellous, isn't it?' I said.

It was the beginning of June. Goose Green had fallen a few days before and British troops were encamped on Mount Kent, overlooking Port Stanley. It seemed that in a matter of hours the battle for the Falklands would be over. But if I'd stopped to think I'd have known my mother wasn't referring to that. So uninterested were my parents in those epic events that if I'd used the word 'war' they'd more than likely have asked which one.

'Marvellous,' my father echoed, derisively. I should also have known he would be on the line, for my parents only used the telephone in tandem. To my mother, he then added, 'I told you he didn't care. *Shagetz*!'

'Obviously he hasn't heard, have you Danny?' my mother said, addressing us both simultaneously.

'Don't tell me someone's broken your car aerial

again,' I said. 'Give me a minute to get some things together and we can all flee the country.'

'See,' my father said, followed by a stream of epithets which sounded like interference on the line.

'If you want to talk to each other,' I said, 'you don't need me. It's late, and I'm tired. So if you don't mind ...'

'Really, you haven't heard?' Now my mother sounded incredulous.

'He already said he didn't. He's been out with his *Goyische* friends, no doubt.'

'Daniel has nice friends.'

'If you must know, I've been taking a class. So please tell me what you want. I'm hungry and I want to go to bed.'

'Tiredness, hunger? What does he know of those things? When I was a boy ...'

'Don't go on,' I said. 'If it was that good, why did you come to England? I'll tell you: because otherwise we'd all be lampshades now, that's why.'

Ordinarily I wouldn't have thought, let alone said, such a thing – not to my father, anyway. Now, like the ringleader of a failed coup, I awaited the inevitable retribution.

'You heard him,' my father said, his voice quavering. 'That I should live to see the day a son of mine ...'

'Dad, it was a joke!'

There was a click on the line. In a subdued voice, my mother said, 'Danny. Danny, darling.

You mustn't say such things, not even in jest. Your father. His family. Our family. What they did ... never joke about it.'

'I know. I'm sorry. You know I don't mean anything,' I said. 'Why does he have to take it all personally?'

'So he thinks it doesn't mean anything! So I'll tell him ...' My father had surreptitiously returned, his forces replenished. 'Go on,' he instructed my mother. 'Tell the ... the Nazi what's been happening. Out there. Tonight. In the real world. Not in any stupid studio.'

Out there. The real world. It could mean only one thing: Israel.

'Oh, shit, not another war,' I said blithely. 'So who's getting their teeth kicked in this time? Now I know why there're so many Jewish dentists!'

Like most Jews with little or no religious faith living in the diaspora, I got a big kick out of Israeli military successes. The occasional, painful reversal, like the massacre of Israeli athletes at the Munich Olympics, was admittedly less thrilling. But it was also not the end of the world.

'Here,' he said, 'in this Arab-owned country you're so proud of, a tragedy has taken place, a monstrous, terrible thing ...' My father's voice shook, his tone became apocalyptic. He began to quote from the Scriptures, fortunately in Hebrew, which I didn't understand.

'There's been a terrorist attack,' my mother put in, matter-of-factly, while my father babbled in the background. 'Schlomo Argov, the ambassa-

127

dor, has been shot. At the Dorchester.'

The note of respect in her voice when she mentioned the name of the hotel was unmistakable.

'Dead?' I said.

'They don't say. But I expect so.'

'He should have known better than to eat in an Arab-owned hotel,' said my father. 'He could have been poisoned.'

So that's what all the fuss was about, I thought. On my way home from school the bus had driven down Park Lane, and traffic had been at a standstill from Hyde Park Corner to Marble Arch.

'So now he knows,' my father said. Then, addressing me directly, 'I suppose you're proud of yourself, you, you ...' and he began to cough uncontrollably.

'That's enough,' my mother said, though I wasn't sure whom she was addressing. 'He's sorry for what he said. Aren't you Danny?'

'If you say so,' I said.

To bring the conversation to an end, I then mumbled a brief apology, but when my father failed to respond I hung up.

Like my father, I had none of the Wilkinsons' reserves of detachment and discretion on which to rely in our long-drawn-out war; nor, to my mother's acute embarrassment, was any time ever wasted in keeping our exchanges private. To her, personal feelings were no more to be paraded in public than were possessions. My sister hadn't strayed from the expected path. She was married to a 'nice' man, a successful retailer who drove a fancy German car, spoilt his children and went on expensive holidays to exotic places. But that was not enough for my parents. I was their only son, and as much the apple of my mother's eye as I was the speck of grit in my father's.

Unlike my mother, who believed it was only a matter of time before I was world famous, my father was more than ready for me to fail. Since my first day at art school, fifteen years before, he had been expecting me to see the light, drop what I was doing and go to work with him. By 'with' he, of course meant 'for' him, but as he said: 'With? For? What's the difference? It'll be yours some day, so better you start now.' To him it was unthinkable that I might not want to, for though far from stupid he couldn't imagine how I preferred what I was doing to an idyllic life spent traipsing down to the warehouse each morning to measure out bolts of cloth, fill in order forms, check invoices, chase up debts and deliveries – all the day-to-day toing and froing of a small businessman in the *schmutter* trade. Not that he saw it that way. After all, he was the boss, the guardian-angel of all those he employed at minimum wages. And then, he had an answer to everything. If I'd made the mistake of suggesting he might have expanded the business a little, he'd have retorted: 'Small? So what's wrong with small? Small is beautiful, as the book says. So we're not M & S. Small gave me a living, a decent living, small gave us all this, permitted you to do as you please. So who are you to talk, you, with your pictures, and your *shiksas* ...?'

At my first show, while my beaming mother confused the abundance of freeloaders with clients, my father jealously kicked his heels. As usual, what he didn't understand he criticised, and when he'd done enough of that he dragged my mother off to the bridge club – bridge being, for many Jews of their generation, merely the continuation of war by other means.

My parents were haunted by the past in a way I couldn't understand, torn between relief that I hadn't had to endure what they'd been through and fear of what they perceived as my unpreparedness for the future. Unacquainted with history – by which my father, naturally, meant Jewish history – I had allowed myself to be lulled into forgetfulness, dropping my guard against a future composed not of 'ifs' but 'whens'. Sometimes I felt he resented me for not having suffered, but to compete over bad experience seemed ridiculous. It reminded me of Duncan bragging about the number of times he'd been caned at school.

During school holidays I'd sometimes gone with my father to the office and watched him doing business. For him it was a place in which his anger and frustration might be legitimately expressed: a hostile, nerve-racking environment in which he felt more at home than ever he could in the spick and span surroundings produced for him by my mother. Despite its appearance – perhaps because of it – their pebble-dashed mock-Tudor house, with its few choice objects on display like so many sporting trophies, was false, unreliable, untrustworthy, illusory.

As my father got older he turned to religion, to the ceremonial and social aspects of it at least, spending Saturday mornings with his cronies at the local *schul*, and celebrating every conceivable high holiday and festival with the grandchildren in whom he hoped to instil that sense of history which had so conspicuously eluded me. Of that world I knew little and believed less, and the first night of Passover, reluctantly spent at my sister's house, was the extent of my hypocrisy.

My mother liked to think that in the fullness of time I would return to my roots, marry a Jewish girl, settle down in Jewish North London and raise a family. It was her version of the family business and however contradictory the evidence, it was one picture I was unable to modify.

As June wore on I had less and less time to myself. In the weeks before the diploma show activity at school was non-stop. Studios had to be emptied and painted, projects quickly brought to an end; the portfolios of foundation students had to be assembled and organised, bad work weeded out before their interviews began; third-year students needed help arranging their exhibitions; prizes and scholarships had to be discussed and awarded. In the middle of the month I dropped Mrs Wilkinson a note to explain why I hadn't been in touch and received by return a charming card telling me not to worry about the portrait. Perhaps, as Janet suggested, I was unconsciously trying to wriggle off that uncomfortable hook.

With so much going on I had little time for social life and hardly saw a newspaper, but to keep informed I could always rely on my mother's breathless bulletins on the progress of 'Operation Peace in Galilee' – as the Israeli invasion of Lebanon was quaintly titled – and my father's furious denunciations of the world's press. I should perhaps have paid more attention to what was happening and how it was being reported. In contrast to the brief, uninformative bulletins and occasional, much-delayed film from the Falklands, scenes of the carnage in Lebanon were in every newspaper and on nearly every news broadcast. But in truth I was too busy to want to know. One war a year was quite enough for me.

When school closed down for the summer vacation I prepared to return to France. But every time I went into the studio the portrait of Mr Wilkinson was like a finger wagging at me. A primed canvas, a few sketchy pencil lines, a group of blown-up black-and-white photographs pinned to the notice-board – such was the extent of my endeavour. But I had to get the job done if I wanted to go abroad, for the summer vacation had to be paid for somehow. So reluctantly and with little feeling I stuck the canvas back on to the easel and went to work, hampered not least by a growing sense that there was something I wanted to say. If I hadn't cared at all, painting Mr Wilkinson's portrait would have been a damn sight easier.

5

There were no two ways about it: I was stuck, and
the harder I tried to free myself of preconce-
ptions about Mr Wilkinson the more I seemed to
caricature him as the bluff old buffer of Jamie's
embittered imagination.

God knows why I'd accepted the commission in
the first place. Perhaps I'd been afraid of
disappointing Mrs Wilkinson, for it would have
been churlish to refuse what was on the face of it
a relatively straightforward job. No painting, of
course, is ever easy. Most of the photographs I'd
received had been taken for publicity or at public
occasions, and revealed little of the private man
behind the practised, plastic smile. Perhaps, too,
I perceived some truth in Jamie's contention that
his father's solid and sensible public persona had
swallowed up the more irascible and domi-
neering private man. Gerald Wilkinson had been
larger than life, though hardly as obtrusive as
Jamie made out, but how was I to convey that
without simply letting him fill the canvas? I'd a
good visual memory and thought I knew just

how to put him across. But portraiture calls for specialised skills and tricks, and my decision to emphasise the informality and intimacy of the pose by draping a tennis jersey round his shoulders – a reference to the sight of him celebrating his victory over Jamie – was a conventional, old-fashioned touch which smacked more of desperation than inspiration.

A few days at Janet's parents' cottage in Sussex did nothing to alleviate my frustration or anxiety, and I was still bogged down when, late one morning in the last week of June, I was surprised by an urgent knocking on the studio door, and even more, by the sight of Duncan himself, standing under an umbrella in a pair of mirrored sunglasses.

There was no point asking how he'd found me. Duncan was a compulsive collector of facts about people and, correspondingly secretive about himself, would never have revealed his source – even if, as was likely, he'd got my address from Jamie. But short of closing the door in his face, and probably not even then, I knew I wouldn't be able to keep him out; also, that before I found out what he wanted we would have to go through an extended game of cat-and-mouse intended to increase his self-importance at my expense. Like the dealer who can't stop negotiating even when he has nothing to sell, Duncan loved to make a mystery where none existed. To admit to having made a journey just to see me, even if he had been capable of such disinterestedness, would have been to endow me with quite unacceptable power. Duncan, as everyone who knew him must have understood, refused to appear dependent on anyone.

Still, much as I resented him, I couldn't but envy his ability always to be himself. Such obliviousness to the feelings and opinions of others was as remarkable as it was infuriating.

Once Duncan had insinuated himself into the studio I left him to it. Sooner or later he would get round to stating his purpose, and the surest way of finding out was to pretend he wasn't there. So while he nosed about the place, making the occasional remark to which I deliberately failed to respond, I carried on with my work.

For no good reason I assumed that her husband's portrait was a matter between Mrs Wilkinson and me, so I was dismayed when, out of the blue, Duncan remarked that I didn't seem to be making much progress with it. Then he moved to one side and I saw he was looking at some preparatory drawings I'd made of Mr Wilkinson which were pinned to the wall.

Affecting a casualness I was far from feeling, I said: 'I'm not complaining. Squaring up's a bit of a chore, but once I get going I'll be OK.'

'Even so, it can't be easy working from photos. You must be rather limited in what you can do.'

One of the things which most irritated me about Duncan was his propensity for saying things from which it was impossible to withhold admiration; in his heavy-handed way he was at times nothing if not acute.

'It's unimaginative, if that's what you mean,' I said. 'More like filling in. But sometimes one doesn't have any choice.'

'You can't very well pose when you're dead, can you?' he said, with a hollow chuckle.

'Most people can't be bothered to sit long enough for a decent portrait when they're alive. They haven't the patience.'

Thanks to the Wilkinsons I'd received, over the years, countless commissions from comfortable, middle-class parents to draw their horrible children, and I knew how hard it was to get them to sit still for more than a minute without resorting to bribery or blackmail.

'I expect they feel defenceless. I know I would,' Duncan said.

Against my will I felt myself being drawn into the kind of conversation I most wanted to avoid, so to cut it short I said: 'Well, anyway, I don't anticipate any real problems. I've drawn him often enough. I could probably do it from memory.'

'Really?' Duncan said. 'I've always thought I'd like a picture of old man Wilkinson.'

'What for?'

'He was one of the great influences on my life.'

Duncan said this with such gravity that I wanted to laugh, but he was beginning to get on my nerves, and I said: 'I'm glad he had such a profound effect on you, but you didn't come here just to pass the time of day.'

'You're quite right. There is something I want to ask.' He glanced at his watch. 'Look,' he added, 'it's not yet half past. How about a snifter? I need your advice.'

Advice? Need? I was certain now that he was up to something, and said: 'Can't you ask me now?'

'I haven't had breakfast.'

'All right. But no more than fifteen minutes,' I said, grateful for the opportunity to get out. 'Then I really must work.'

'It won't take long, I promise.'

'Give me a minute to switch things off,' I said.

'See you in the pub over the road,' he said, not bothering to wait for me.

After he'd gone I stood for a few moments in the middle of the room staring at nothing in particular and conscious of how angry I was feeling, with myself quite as much as with Duncan. Then, buttoning up my bomber-jacket, I switched off the lights and hurried down the stairs.

'What's on your mind?' I asked, as I waited fruitlessly for Duncan to buy me a drink.

Now he had me there he wasn't going to be rushed and after a few moments glanced up from a mountainous plate of shepherd's pie and, with his mouth full, said: 'Not having anything?'

'Duncan. You know I'm busy.'

'No, really. This is great. Try some.'

'I have been here before.'

It wasn't that I was at a loss for words; I knew

exactly what I wanted to say, but my words made no impact. It was the verbal equivalent of the 'Star Wars' project: he hoped to destroy all incoming ideas before they reached their targets, while I hoped that by launching enough some were bound to get through.

I went to the bar for a drink and a sandwich. When I sat down again Duncan said, 'You'll be interested to hear I'm going away.'

'So what's new?'

He pushed his plate to one side. 'Frankly, I was well out of the Falklands. By all accounts it was no picnic.'

'The *QE2* wasn't on a luxury cruise,' I said.

'Still, it's panned out all right.'

I could tell he was waiting for me to question him, so I lit a cigarette and said nothing.

'Yes, something much more interesting has turned up. You won't believe it, but I'm off to Israel, of all places.'

'I believe it,' I said.

'I've wangled the advance on a book. You know, a jumble of personal impressions and political analysis, the usual old thing.'

I knew exactly what he meant. He'd done the same for some of the world's other 'trouble spots': instant-history books, cobbled together in no time by a team of three or four journalists, more concerned with deadlines than depth.

'As you know,' Duncan went on, 'there's already a widespread movement against Israeli imperialism within the country itself.'

'A bit different from the Falklands, when anyone who spoke up was branded a traitor,' I said.

'I don't remember much of that from you,' he said. 'I know you won't believe it, but they'd been planning to invade Lebanon for months. All that stuff about cross-border attacks was bullshit. There haven't been any in more than a year. Which is why the PLO denied trying to assassinate Argov. They knew Sharon would use it as a pretext.'

'The Israelis shot their own ambassador, I suppose!'

'I wouldn't put it past them.'

I couldn't see what any of this had to do with me, but I was beginning to feel uncomfortable, and said: 'I thought you wanted my advice about something.'

For a moment Duncan looked embarrassed. He opened his mouth and seemed about to speak. Then he picked up his empty glass, asked if I wanted another and went over to the bar. As he sat down again he said: 'Remember that time we went to see *Cabaret*? At some fleapit in Camden Town.'

'King's Cross,' I said.

'You got rather upset.'

'Don't you remember what you said?'

'The film was rather good, wasn't it?'

'I hated it,' I said.

'You shouldn't be so sensitive. It was only a film.'

I still had no idea what this was leading up to

and said, in exasperation: 'What do you want?'

'Dan, I know you think I'm insensitive, but you should know that some of the things you've said in the past have wounded me deeply.'

'Like hell!'

'On that occasion something I said seemed to annoy you.'

'And...'

'Well, I just want you to know that if it makes any difference I didn't mean anything, you know, by what I said ...'

'Whatever it was.'

'Yes, whatever it was.'

'It doesn't.'

We finished our beer in silence. For once Duncan seemed at a loss for words. Finally, less out of curiosity than boredom, I said: 'So now you're off to Israel?'

'Yes, and the thing is, I don't know any Jews.'

'That doesn't surprise me,' I said, recalling his joke about gas-chambers which had upset me all those years ago, which even now made me furious whenever I thought of it.

'Don't get me wrong,' he quickly added. 'I'm not writing about Jews, but about Israelis.'

Even in my most paranoid fantasies I hadn't expected that. Every Jew knows there are only two ways of being a Jew: if your mother is Jewish or, like Sammy Davies Jr or Elizabeth Taylor, by conversion. Duncan, nevertheless, seemed to believe that being an Israeli and a Jew were two distinct things. As my father might have said, had the subject come up, 'So Hitler didn't gas any Israelis. That makes him a Righteous Gentile, I suppose?'

'The thing is,' Duncan said, 'I'm putting together a list of names and addresses of people to talk to, and you're my only Jewish friend.'

'Surely not?'

'I can't think of anyone else.'

'Get on with it,' I said.

'There are plenty of official sources, of course, but what I want are ordinary people.'

'Like me, you mean?'

'You often talk about your father, how he's become all religious.'

'Try him.'

'You think he might help?'

'Not if you tell him you're a friend of mine. Anyway, he doesn't converse with the Goyim.'

'Still, there must be someone you can put me in touch with.'

I stared at him, wondering how seriously to take this nonsense, and then said: 'Duncan, you're winding me up.'

'Of course not. Why should I?'

'Because it's your favourite occupation. As we say at Passover, "*Mah Nishtanah Halilah Hazeh* – why is this day different from all other days?"' It was astonishing. I only had to be in Duncan's company for a few minutes to feel I ought to be wearing ringlets and a fur hat and living in Stamford Hill. 'This may come as a surprise to you,' I said, 'but I've never been to Israel. Nor, as

142

far as I know, do I have any relations living there. So you can stop pretending and tell me your real reasons for dragging me here?'

'What else could I possibly want?'

'You're up to something. I know it.'

'You people always look for the worst in others.'

'In your case that's not difficult.'

'Look, if you don't want to help me ...'

'But your mind's already made up. You're only looking to confirm your prejudices? Why should I help do that?'

I thought at that moment of my father and how I might easily have said the same to him. The idea of the two meeting made me smile, briefly.

I could see Duncan was no longer interested in what I had to say, but I nevertheless seemed to have a continuing need to explain myself, or at least to get something off my chest, and as I stood up to leave, I said: 'I realise that to people like you I've no hope of being considered English, my loyalties being in question and all that, but I'll give you a piece of advice for nothing: once you're over there, you'll soon find that the English aren't exactly flavour of the month. So if I were you I'd keep my head down and my mouth shut. Unlike here, they don't give a shit where you went to school or which crappy club you belong to.'

I telephoned Jamie as soon as I got back to the studio. 'You won't believe what Duncan's just asked,' I said, describing what had taken place.

When I finished I waited for his reaction. 'Well?' I said, when he failed to respond. 'Have you ever heard such *chutzpah*? Who on earth could have suggested it?' But before I'd even finished the question, I realised I already knew the answer.

'I did, as a matter of fact,' he said.

'But why?'

'If it had been anyone else you'd have helped, wouldn't you?'

'What makes you think I was in any position to?'

'Oh, I don't know. I suppose I just thought ...'

'That one Jew's as good as another? Christ, Jamie, you know stacks more useful people than I do. I mean, your father was even a Labour Friend of Israel, whatever that is.'

'I expect I could have done something, got him some useful contacts, but I didn't want him pestering me. You know how remorseless he is, and I've far more important things on my plate. Anyway, I've got to be careful these days, asking favours. I don't want to put anyone's back up before I'm in the House.'

When he said this I wondered in what way he imagined things would change if he was ever elected to Parliament, but somehow the words wouldn't come. So after a few moments I told him I had to get back to work and put the phone down.

6

I returned to France at the beginning of August. My first batch of drawings of the wine country had been well received, and I'd been asked for more. As usual, I was happy to get away from England, and I took advantage of good weather to do some drawing for myself – sketches and impressions which might later be worked up into something in the studio – if, that is, I was ever done with Mr Wilkinson's portrait, which I'd rashly promised for the autumn.

I worked out of doors in the warm, soft air and most evenings went to bed straight after dinner. When I'd finished in Bordeaux I planned to drive around France with Janet and to meet that deadline allowed me few distractions.

While in France I missed the return of the Fleet from the South Atlantic. Once British troops had landed on the Falklands much of the suspense had seemed to evaporate, and that extraordinary episode, about which I'd once felt so enthusiastic, already seemed remote. On my previous visit to France I'd found myself the butt of incessant facetious remarks from people both amused and bemused by Margaret Thatcher. Now another, more serious, war had replaced that campaign, one with which I was glad not to be closely identified; and where earlier I had relished the roles of spokesman and interpreter of English behaviour I preferred a silence for which work provided the best excuse.

I felt ashamed of what was happening in Lebanon. I'd swallowed Israeli propaganda about PLO 'provocations' because I was used to reading of terrorist outrages and other 'incidents' in which words like 'innocent' and 'responsible' were rendered meaningless by 'spokesmen' and guilt by association was raised to a governing principle. Now that Israeli forces were embarked on a full-scale invasion of Lebanon, indiscriminately bombing cities and civilian populations, I, like many other Jews, was obliged to open my eyes.

I take no active interest in politics. Though I read the papers to keep myself informed, I don't for one moment think I can change anything. But if I could provide no answers to what was happening in the Middle East, sufficient even to satisfy myself, no one else seemed to either. As usual, my father insisted I didn't know what I was talking about, but I suspected I knew as much, or as little, as he did: the Palestinian Arabs were a displaced, unwanted people who would not 'disappear', as so many had in Argentina – that was the issue no one was prepared to tackle without resorting to force. Of course, I believed in the right of Israel to exist, as I believe my easel remains standing there when I turn my back on it – there seems no point pretending otherwise. What I couldn't help feeling, and what my father's exuberance seemed only to confirm, was that the Palestinians had become the new Jews of the Middle East: unwanted, maligned, oppressed, contained, in much the same way as Jews had been for centuries.

We returned home at the end of August when my parents were themselves abroad and I was thankfully spared their nightly bulletins on the latest triumph of Israeli might. For weeks on end newspapers and television screens were filled with the carnage: rubble, bodies and the names of places I'd only read in history books or heard of from my Hebrew teacher twenty years before. But my father, who had shown not the slightest interest in the invasion of the Falklands, and who dismissed the horrific casualties out of hand as anti-semitic propaganda, found in the Lebanese war a legitimate outlet for all his animosity towards the world. Someone else was getting it in the neck, and not before time.

True to form, my mother was less sanguine, for her antennae were always honed to pick up signals of impending outrage. A swastika daubed on a motorway bridge, the news that some long-lost Nazi was occupying a high-flying job or training the paramilitary in some banana republic, was enough to set her to packing

147

suitcases. For her, history had a habit of repeating itself, and if now wasn't the turn of the Jews it most certainly soon would be.

My parents returned from their holiday, but I couldn't face the thought of seeing them. Every day the news was worse, and every day I cooked up some excuse to stay away. I particularly dreaded meeting my father. I hoped that by now he had come to his senses, but he had always been pig-headed. He felt that a Jew's first duty was to defend Israel, as one might protect a child – some child! – and if I couldn't see that I wasn't a proper Jew. But a Jew, come what may, I remained. People like Duncan would always see to that.

Bob Rosen, no more observant a Jew than I, half-humorously accused me of 'assimilationist tendencies', when losing my identity was the last thing I wanted. What I didn't need was for other people to tell me who I was. I was an artist: not a 'Jewish artist', or an 'English artist', not necessarily a good artist, but an artist none the less – someone defined by his way of looking at the world. It was the only way I could take myself seriously and be effective, and in my studio I felt more at home than I ever had in my parents' house.

After three weeks I'd run out of excuses and could no longer postpone letting my parents see me. It was also their wedding anniversary, and a table had been booked at their favourite Italian restaurant. My father made clear his intention to live it up, so I was appointed chauffeur for the evening and instructed to collect him from the club in which, on a couple of afternoons a week, he and his cronies abused one another over the bridge table. With its bright lights and brash wallpaper, angry voices and infantile tantrums, it could hardly have been further removed from Jamie's gloomy sanctuary in Pall Mall.

I arrived at six-thirty to find my mother, dressed to the nines, perched at my father's elbow, surrounded by old codgers and cigar smoke. Though she played a damn sight better than he did, it was a sensible rule of the club that husband and wife should never play at the same table. I glanced at the score to see how long we were likely to wait and then wandered off. When I returned, my father was exactly as I'd left him, considering his lead into dummy. Beside me a squat, middle-aged man with slicked-down hair and a sparkling diamond ring, jabbed my arm with his finger. 'Bridge,' he confided at the top of his voice, 'it's an easy game so long as you make up your mind. Hesitate, and you're finished.' I don't know why he'd picked on me. Perhaps he didn't care whom he was addressing. When I tried to move away he nudged me again and cocked his chin in the direction of another table. 'Bertie Wooster over there,' he said, indicating a complacent-looking young man in tweeds: 'play with him, you might as well be home in bed. Yes', he added, turning back to my father's table, 'there's nothing difficult about bridge so long as you make up your mind. With old Jo here, we could all be in our graves before he decides what to play.'

At that moment my mother glanced anxiously at me and whispered: 'He's had terrible cards all afternoon.'

'He's always said life dealt him a bad hand,' I said.

'Danny, please. No jokes. Not tonight.'

'What did he say?' my father said, without taking his eyes off his cards.

'Nothing, Jo. You just carry on.'

'What do you think I'm trying to do? All these interruptions! A person hasn't the chance to think.'

'What's to think?' declarer said. 'Lead!'

'You play a card, it's wrong, it's not the end of the world,' said my father's partner.

'I'm thinking', my father said, gazing blankly at his cards, 'the whole game depends on what I do.'

'Jo, if your aunt had balls she'd be your uncle.'

'He obviously never met Maidie,' I said.

'Don't think. Play.'

My father removed and folded his spectacles. He peered up at the ceiling. He frowned and raised his eyebrows. He crossed, uncrossed and recrossed his legs. Then at last, glaring triumphantly, he yanked out a card.

Long before the hand was played out the recriminations began.

'All along you had the four of Spades,' said his incredulous partner, 'and still you lead the Jack?

You're playing with a partner here.' To the table, he then added: 'It's always the same. He plays like a novice.'

'He makes a muckery!'

'Top of nothing,' my father said, cutting the cards.

'Nothing up top, you mean! You shouldn't even sit down at the table. With the four in his hand he leads the Jack! *Ausgezeichnet!*'

My father began to sort his new hand. Not a point anywhere. He looked at his cards, looked at his partner, looked at his cards again. Then, leaning heavily against my mother for support, he pulled himself out of his chair.

'Ach, you're all so clever, you play,' he said, chucking his cards onto the table. 'Come on. I'm hungry,' he told my mother, and amid the sudden commotion the three of us retreated rapidly from the room.

I couldn't tell if my father had been drinking. Usually he took only tea and a piece of cake when he was playing. But he was in a thoroughly bad mood, and as soon as we were outside he turned on me, demanding to know where the car was.

'Round the corner. Less than two minutes' walk,' I said, glancing at my mother.

'You fetch it,' he said. 'I'll wait.'

'Come on, Jo,' my mother said, taking his arm. 'The exercise will do you good. You've been sitting all afternoon.'

'You want to walk, go with him. I'm staying.'

So I went off on my own to collect the car, after

which we drove to the Trattoria in silence.

My father loved the sound and fury of Italian restaurants. He imagined the effusiveness and exaggerated affection with which he was greeted was reserved for him alone, and revelled in playing the paterfamilias, pinching his grand-children's cheeks and telling everyone what they should eat. It fostered an illusion of generosity and authority. Here people listened to him and loved him, he believed. But this evening something was different, and even the manager, with whom my father was on familiar, back-slapping terms, was treated more like a stranger than the usual long-lost brother.

My sister's family were seated at table when we arrived, the children dressed up in party clothes, my sister in a new hair-do and plenty of flashy jewellery, and while she tried to cheer up the old man I abandoned my resolution to give up smoking and cadged a cigarette from my brother-in-law.

'What's up with him?' he whispered, almost setting my moustache alight with his solid gold lighter. 'He doesn't seem his normal self.'

'Fat chance!' I said. 'He's had bad cards all afternoon.'

'It's not the cards,' my mother explained. 'Your father's upset. We all are.'

Everyone sounded so gloomy, I was beginning to feel I'd been asked under false pretences. All too accurately the underwater feel of the grotto-like room seemed to mirror my relationship with my family.

A waiter nearby clicked his tongue. My mother said, 'There's been a massacre. It was on the news. Women and children, hundreds dead, in one of those camps. And already they're blaming us.'

'He knows that,' my sister said, 'or he doesn't want to know.'

'You'd think a thing like that would cheer Dad up,' I said.

At the opposite end of the table my father murmured 'terrorists, murderers of innocent people'.

'No jokes, Dan, please,' my mother said. 'This is serious.'

'Yes. Be serious for once in your life,' my sister chipped in, inspecting her false fingernails.

'It's been serious for months, only he doesn't appear to have noticed,' I said.

'Propaganda. Wicked lies,' my father said. 'The lot of it.'

'This time maybe they've gone too far,' my mother said; then, to the table in general: 'I knew something like this would happen on our anniversary!'

'I'm sure it wasn't deliberate,' I said, smiling. 'The coincidence, I mean', but no one smiled back.

When my father finally made up his mind the waiter took our order. After he had gone my father said: 'Sure it's a sad day. Today we have given the *Goyim* the ammunition they always wanted to make us look to the world like murderers.'

'Some Jews are,' I said, quietly. 'Same as everyone.'

'Naturally it's bad,' my brother-in-law said. 'I won't deny it. But why blame yourself? It's not as if we did it. The *Goyim* did the killing. Everyone knows that.'

'So what's new?' my mother said.

'We're all to blame,' my father said, unexpectedly.

'Speak for yourself,' I said. 'Some of us have been against the war from the start, or haven't you noticed? But I don't suppose you've even heard of "Peace Now". The people you admire so much are a bunch of mad zealots who want to rewrite history, *Meshugganas* and mass-murderers, like any others.'

'We still don't know exactly what happened,' my sister said, wiping invisible crumbs from her daughter's mouth.

'We know,' my father said, again to my surprise.

'Some of us have known for months,' I said.

'Who's a clever boy?' my sister said, grabbing my cheek.

'Your father's right. It must be propaganda,' my mother said. 'It couldn't be as bad as they say.'

'Here,' my father said, tossing the wine list at me. 'You're so clever, you choose.'

My niece and nephew were staring into their laps. My brother-in-law was gazing at the ceiling.

My mother's eyes were on the bread basket, my father's unblinkingly on me. Only my sister seemed prepared to speak to me, and that was to ask, incredulously, 'Seriously, you hadn't heard, you didn't know?'

'His head was always in the clouds,' my mother said.

'My son the fartist!' said my father, provoking giggles from the children.

'Why am I expected to know everything that goes on on the other side of the world?' I asked.

'Israel's hardly the other side of the world!'

'What happens there affects us all,' murmured my mother, mournfully.

'Too true.'

'Quite right.'

'And I suppose everyone in Israel follows what goes on here.'

'It's not the same.'

'Dan can't see that.'

'He doesn't want to.'

'He never could.'

'You mean he can't be bothered.'

'You're quite right', I said, 'I can't see any difference.'

'He's joking,' my mother said.

'Like hell he is,' my father said.

'He always liked to make jokes,' my mother added, as if I was dead.

'You're not serious, are you, Dan?' There was something rather winning in my sister's hopefulness, which made me not want to disappoint her, but something pitying also.

'Pass,' I said, plucking a cigarette from a packet on the table.

By no stretch of the imagination did I come from an educated family – my father had gone to work at fourteen, my sister married almost straight from school – but on one thing they were all experts: Israel. Or, at least, they thought they were. By failing to keep myself informed I was failing in some kind of tribal obligation, failing to identify properly with my people. This was hardly the first time I had been remiss. When the Israeli ambassador had been shot at the beginning of June I had chosen to believe that the invasion of Lebanon was a simple act of retaliation, another lightning response from our glorious citizens' army in the tradition of Entebbe, without considering any of the logistical difficulties of mobilising an army overnight.

Naturally, I had wanted to believe the propaganda, I wanted, like the rest of my family and Jews everywhere, to accept whatever Israel's rulers wanted me to: that the war was merely defensive, retaliatory, pre-emptive: to create a narrow buffer zone in southern Lebanon, to make the northern frontier secure. Now I felt deceived and disappointed, ashamed more of my innocence than my ignorance, and I held my breath, hoping against hope that the widespread destruction and slaughter were no more than the mendacious, anti-semitic propaganda my father insisted upon. The truth, as anyone could see, was that Israel was waging an aggressive, imperialist war like any other; the shame that her leaders had not the courage to admit what they were doing.

'A few years back the same thing happened. No one blamed us then,' my brother-in-law chipped in.

'That's because we hadn't yet invaded,' I said.

'So it's "we" now, is it?' my father said.

'Keep to the point,' I said.

'They say we got the *Goyim* to do our dirty work,' my mother said, 'as if they ever needed encouragement to rape and murder innocent people!'

'Such *chutzpah* I never heard,' my father said. 'Two thousand years we've been doing the jobs they wouldn't touch.'

'I'm not defending them,' I said.

'You're attacking us,' my sister said. 'What's the difference?'

'The way the *Goyim* talk you'd think it was one of their famous garden-parties,' my father said. 'All's fair in love and war, that's what I say.'

'Not women and young children,' muttered my mother.

'Dad!' my sister and I said, momentarily united.

I didn't expect my family to agree with me. As I say, each of them was, in his own way, more involved in being Jewish than I was. But at that celebratory dinner, as I looked into all the faces round that sad, subdued table, it was as clear as

157

day that the game of bluff was up, that with the news of Sabra and Chatilla this was the last opportunity to decide where one stood. Anyone who couldn't see that now never would.

I wanted my father to come to his senses. The excitement, exhilaration, exultation he had felt in putting his enemies to the sword, his joy in rampant Judaism, was terrifying in its purity. The cowering ghetto Jew of his parents' and grandparents' time, living in perpetual shadow, had been avenged; the might of Israel was fulfilling by proxy his nastiest fantasies. But there was nothing romantic about what was happening now. This was not the stuff of Hollywood, of Entebbe, Exodus or David and Goliath. As my father had remarked apropos of atomic weapons, 'Whether they like it or not, we've joined the club. And they can't do a thing about it.'

Throughout the meal my father hardly spoke, and if anyone tried to cheer him up would turn on them, angry and bewildered. His expectations of Israel had always been excessive. That his suspension of disbelief should have led him to take up untenable positions, as fortified and useless as the Maginot Line, now rendered him speechless. And, as usual, when he had nothing to say, he spoke loudest.

'It was a just war,' he said, to no one in particular, at the end of the meal. 'A holy war. *Milhemet Mitzva*. According to the Talmud, he who begins a *Mitzva* must also end it.'

'Killing never solves anything.'

'If the Rabbis say so, who am I to disagree?'

' "They would, wouldn't they?" as that famous Israeli war hero Mandy Rice Davies said.'

My father stared straight through me. 'All this talk of legitimate frontiers, who's to say what's legitimate? Do the terrorists respect borders? All they understand is force. Read the Constitution. It's all there. Israel never had borders. Ben Gurion, Golda Meir, they all knew. As the scriptures say, Judea and Sammaria...'

'Dad, the Bible's fiction.'

'Every word is true,' he said.

This was the last straw. Despite the faces my mother was pulling to make me desist, and my sister's manicured hand on my sleeve, I refused to let that pass. How would my father, who had spent the best part of his life *schlepping* between Finchley and Oxford Street, feel if a Roman or a Saxon or a Viking appeared on his doorstep to reclaim his ancestral home? Looking one after the other into the faces of my family, I saw every emotion except love, and felt, not for the first time, like a stranger. Without saying a word I stood up, dropped the car keys onto the table and walked out of the restaurant.

I wanted to get home as fast as possible, driven by a perverse desire to hear not just the news, but the worst news possible.

'I meant to tell you, your hero rang earlier,' Janet said. 'He sounded rather upset.'

159

I was sunk in an armchair, drink in hand, scowling at the television set. Without looking up, I said: 'His name will do.'

'He is still your friend, isn't he?'

'Of course. I owe him a lot,' I said. 'Did he say what he wanted?'

'You don't think he'd tell me?'

'You mean you didn't ask.'

'Of course I did. He said he'd a number of calls to make and he'd try again later.'

'But why didn't you tell me?' I said. I had by now been at home for more than an hour.

'I was busy. I forgot. Does it matter?'

'And how many other messages do you choose not to pass on?'

'Dozens. Every day. Thousands. I'm not a bloody answering service,' she said. 'You were in such a foul mood when you came in it was safer to leave you alone.'

'But he's probably gone out by now.'

'If you're that concerned, ring him.'

'I don't feel like it,' I said.

But when the news was over I did try Jamie's number. Constantly engaged, it was only after midnight when I was pretty plastered that I finally got through to him, and Jamie told me he'd heard from a friend in the embassy in Tel Aviv that a British journalist answering Duncan's description had been reported killed when the helicopter in which he was travelling was shot down over southern Lebanon.

160

7

Ten days after Duncan's funeral I received an invitation from Jamie. It was fitting, he wrote, that Duncan's many friends should have an opportunity to get together, but regrettably the size of the room he had hired obliged him to keep numbers down. To avoid having to exclude anyone who wished to attend, an immediate reply was requested.

I couldn't see the point of such a gathering so soon after the event, but if it was something Jamie wanted, who was I to interfere? I'd been busy finishing his father's portrait and hadn't so much as seen or spoken to him since the funeral. When I called to thank him for the invitation and I asked what he had in mind for the evening, he was characteristically vague. Before hanging up he said, quite unnecessarily, that he hoped I wouldn't let him down.

The invitation stipulated seven-thirty for eight o'clock and when I arrived at the club I recognised one or two people standing in the entrance-hall. One person was wearing a dinner jacket, another a double-breasted suit, and when we were shown into the private dining-room, glittering and glimmering with silverware and candlelight, I was greatly relieved to see I wasn't alone in not having dressed up.

From the look of the room it was obvious Jamie had spared no expense. A bar was set up in front of a row of overvarnished military portraits, and as soon as I'd been relieved of my coat I was presented with a glass of champagne. There must have been half a dozen glasses beside each place-setting as well as a specially printed menu, but there were no name-cards on the long, highly-polished table, and when dinner was announced Jamie invited us to sit where we liked. After the usual to-ing and fro-ing I took the chair on Jamie's left, while the one on his right remained empty.

The first course passed in almost complete silence, and the plates had just been cleared away when Bob appeared through a door at the far end of the room. Even at a distance it was obvious he was pissed. As he weaved his way round the table, stopping every so often for a word in someone's ear or to support himself – it wasn't clear which – I glanced anxiously at Jamie. When Bob at last reached us, he bowed in a caricature of formality, slumped down in the empty chair and helped himself to wine.

Jamie seemed in no way put out by this intrusion. In fact I couldn't help admiring his insouciance. It hadn't occurred to me that Bob would be asked, for in my surprise at seeing him I'd forgotten that he and Duncan had occasionally worked together. Taking the decanter from Bob, Jamie filled his glass for him and said: 'I've saved you some first course. Otherwise you're just in time for the beef.'

'If it's all the same to you, I'm not hungry,' Bob said. 'Wine's all I need.'

'We've noticed,' someone muttered. I don't think Bob heard, nor would he have cared, but Jamie seemed momentarily uneasy and glanced at me in a way which suggested he would hold me responsible if anything went wrong.

Although Bob had always been a heavy drinker, it hardly seemed to interfere with his intelligence. When he was plastered his mind was razor sharp – too much so for his own good perhaps. But there was no point trying to control him. As with most drunks, the best one could hope was for him to get side-tracked, lose interest, even fall asleep. Unfortunately he seemed unlikely to do any of these, and after a few minutes said loudly: 'Why isn't anyone saying anything? That's what we're here for, isn't it? To talk about jolly old Duncan. To share the experience, as the lightbulb said to the analyst ... or is it the other way round ...?'

'Eat something first,' Jamie suggested.

'If you insist,' Bob said and, when Jamie wasn't looking, winked at me as if to say: does he really think he can subdue me that easily?

Everyone had finished eating by the time Bob

was served, and it was obvious from people's faces that they were expecting trouble. Although there was a good deal of quiet conversation round the table, no one seemed ready to initiate any kind of public discussion, but as the subject had been raised, I didn't see how Jamie could avoid it.

'So who's going to start the ball rolling?' Bob announced. With a clatter he put down his knife and fork and stared straight at me.

'Why not you?' Jamie said. 'You obviously want to.' Then, turning to the table, he added, though I didn't believe he meant it for a moment: 'Everyone should have the chance to say something. I know Duncan would appreciate that.'

'Me?' Bob said. 'I barely knew him.' But when no one else showed willing it was Bob, not Jamie, who spoke. 'This obviously isn't going to work', he said. 'Let's try another tack. Everyone must have some story to tell about Duncan. How about you, Dan?' he added, turning back to me. 'You had strong feelings about him.'

'Cool it, will you?' I muttered, loud enough for everyone to hear. 'We were having a perfectly good time till you turned up.'

'That's rich, coming from you, after your behaviour at the wake.'

I must have looked dumbfounded. I certainly felt it, for he then said: 'Don't play the innocent, ask your friend here.'

I glanced anxiously at Jamie who, looking

down the table, said: 'We're here for only one reason. To remember Duncan. I wasn't going to say anything, but I now see it's not such a bad idea. Duncan was quite a character. We all know that. So how about starting at the far end and working round? But please don't feel you have to say anything if you don't want to.'

I stared furiously at the table, hardly hearing a word of what was said. I had no idea what Bob was up to. Like everyone else, I had been a bit tight at Duncan's wake, but I wasn't aware of having said or done anything untoward. Moreover it was inconceivable that Jamie would have said anything to Bob about me, for they hated the sight of each other.

When I looked up, someone was telling a story about working with Duncan, a farcical account of royalty-chasing which provoked a good deal of laughter in which I half-heartedly joined. Since Bob's arrival there had been terrific tension in the room. But now, as the general mood lightened, the stories about Duncan became more scurrilous and intimate: someone who had shared a flat with him remarking on his obsessional bathroom routine, another on his unembarrassability.

One or two people declined to say anything, with the excuse that someone else had already told their story, that it would take too long, that others were clearer about the details. So far everything had been inoffensive enough and received with obvious relief. In the mood Bob

165

had put me everything seemed, if anything, a damn sight too restrained. Then a decanter of port arrived in front of me which I handed to the person on my right. Addressing me for the first time since the story-telling had begun, Jamie muttered, 'The other way.'

'Aren't you having any?' I asked.

'That's not the point,' he said.

Bob pulled another face and nodded sagely. The table then went quiet. I glanced up and saw that everyone was staring at me and realised to my horror that it was now my turn to speak.

For the past half hour or so, I had been flipping through my recollections of Duncan in the hope of finding something entertaining to relate. I had memories aplenty, each of which might be made to illuminate some aspect of his personality, but none seemed quite suitable for the occasion. Nor did I necessarily expect anyone else to be amused by what I found funny. But I knew that despite my reluctance I wanted to say something, and hoped that in the solemn faces round the table I might yet find inspiration.

Emptying my glass, I said, 'There is one subject no one's mentioned.' I paused to see if anyone could guess. When no one spoke I went on: 'Perhaps it's not surprising, when one considers how quiet Duncan kept about it. On the other hand, it was always on his mind.' I glanced at Jamie who clearly hadn't a clue what I was referring to. 'What's missing from this gathering? Women, of course.'

'This is a gentleman's club ... isn't it?' Bob said.

'Who for example was the vamp in black, smashed out of her head at the funeral?' When I said this I glanced at Jamie, hoping for a reaction. Since Duncan's funeral I'd been wondering what had caused his delay in getting to the wake. Had he gone back to the churchyard to find the Black Widow or, unknown to me, spotted her in the pub where we'd stopped off en route? Perhaps Jamie was no longer listening, and was only wondering what he'd done to deserve the way, after such careful planning, the evening was turning out. Whatever the case, he continued to stare unblinkingly at his plate, and after a moment or two I looked again down the length of the table and said: 'We all know how interested Duncan was in other people's sex lives, but did you also know he kept lists of people's lovers? He was compiling a chart, a sort of "Who's-fucked-who?", though I don't know how far he got with it.'

'This isn't going anywhere,' Jamie said, looking thoroughly embarrassed.

'What a brilliant idea!' Bob said. 'Christ, if one could only get hold of it! I hardly knew him but it was obvious he was a voyeur. In fact, he was the most frustrated person I've ever met.'

'We're not here to discuss that,' Jamie said.

'We're remembering Duncan, aren't we?' Bob said. He seemed very sober now and I was suddenly nervous of what he might say.

'Let me illustrate what I mean with a little story,' he said.

167

Five or six years before, Bob and Duncan had
been covering the same royal story. They were
staying in a hotel somewhere near Balmoral, and
Bob had come into the bar late one evening to
find Duncan chatting up a very unattractive girl.
Unaware that anyone was watching, Duncan had
become increasingly frantic in his efforts to
impress on her his importance. It was obvious to
Bob that the girl was desperate to escape, so out
of kindness he had joined them. Instead of
introducing her Duncan had then tried to
pretend she had nothing to do with him.

'The point,' Bob said, 'was that Duncan, who so
liked being all things to all men, had been caught
out being himself. He didn't know how long I'd
been watching, not that there was anything to
see, but after that evening he deliberately
avoided me. He'd run a mile whenever I came
into a room! Evidently, he regarded me as a
threat, God knows why! What the hell did I care
who he tried to screw? Also I don't think he cared
whether he got off with her, but pretending had
become habit. He couldn't have admitted the
truth at that moment even if he'd wanted to.'

'He was surprised to see you, I expect,' Jamie
said. 'No one wants everything known about
them. We all have our little weaknesses.'

'Even you?'

'Yes, even me.'

'Well, anyway', Bob added, modestly, 'it was
only an observation. I thought it might ring a few
bells with people who knew him better than I

did.' Then he turned to me and said, 'What do you think Duncan was doing in Israel of all places?'

'Making trouble, I expect. As usual!'

Leaning closer, but not bothering to lower his voice, Bob said, 'It's funny, you know, but a few years back we were covering a story about American bases. There'd been a near-nuclear accident and I was damn sure then he was up to something. There'd been the usual half-arsed cover-up, but Duncan was only too willing to swallow the official line, which wasn't like him at all. The thing is, I could never work out which side he was working for.' Bob smiled. 'It's a game I like to play, trying to imagine which side people one knows would be on if there was an invasion, or we came under the domination of some foreign power. We'd probably all be put up against a wall, but some are bound to survive. Your friend here, for instance,' he said, helping himself to port. 'He'd come through all right. You too, Dan. But Duncan I never had any doubts at all about. He'd have been another Beria.'

'Duncan a spook? Don't make me laugh,' Jamie said.

'He's only joking,' I said, uncertainly.

'Duncan was a very able chap, a lot smarter than he let on. Playing the innocent was only a way of getting people to drop themselves in the shit.'

At eleven o'clock a number of people stood up

169

to go. The dozen or so remaining then moved up to our end of the table. 'Come on,' Bob said, looking from one face to another, 'A number of you worked with him. Someone must have suspected something.'

'Why not?' I said. 'Everyone else at Cambridge seems to have been one!'

'That's quite enough,' Jamie said. 'We're here to remember a friend, a good friend, not to slander him when he can't defend himself.'

'Have it your own way,' Bob said.

'Bob's right,' I heard myself say. 'What the hell was he doing over there? He didn't give a shit about the Jews or Israel. As for his friends, there was nothing he liked more than dropping them in it so he could come to their rescue.'

I sat back and looked apprehensively at the surrounding faces. I realised that this was what I had wanted to say all along but had felt too inhibited to express; without Bob's lead, I wouldn't have had the courage to come out with it.

'Duncan was a bloody good journalist and a bloody good bloke,' said someone three seats away, who hadn't previously spoken. 'That's all there is to it. What's more, you've got a bloody nerve saying those things now. Quite out of order.'

After a few moments I realised I'd seen the speaker before, at one of Duncan's parties: a rugger-bugger type who at some point in the evening had taken a woman by the throat and banged her head against the wall. Not surprisingly this memory only added to my concern that things might yet get out of hand. I had said my piece. Now seemed like a good time to leave. But the rugger-bugger wasn't finished, and as I stood up he ordered me back into my chair.

'I'll tell you what Duncan was doing over there. He was trying to expose what was going on, to get behind the crap put out by the government propaganda machine.'

'Nonsense,' Bob said, reaching for the decanter. 'He was just interested in a good story, like any other hack.'

'There was nothing to expose anyway,' I said. 'It's all been in the papers for weeks.'

'You're drunk,' someone else said.

'We've all had enough,' Jamie said, putting a restraining hand on Bob's sleeve.

'Duncan was a bloody good bloke,' the rugger-bugger said in a voice choked with emotion, 'worth more than the lot of you.'

'I'm not responsible for his death,' Bob said.

'He knew the risks. He didn't have to go,' I suggested. 'I even warned him not to.'

'An accident! Bollocks!' the rugger-bugger said. 'He went because he wanted to get at the truth, which people like you have been trying to hide.'

'Sorry?' I said, suddenly chilly.

'People like who?' Bob asked. 'Oh, now I see.'

'See what?' I said, shooting him an anxious glance.

171

By now I was prepared for almost anything, but even I couldn't have guessed what was coming.

As he lurched to his feet, the rugger-bugger leaned across the table jabbing his finger and said, 'It was you bloody Yids who killed him, same as you wiped out all those refugees. For years we've been hearing how hard done by you are, with your flash cars and fancy houses. Well, we're sick to death of it, d'you hear, sick of being told how much you've suffered, and how much the world owes you. Because it doesn't owe you a bloody thing. From now on no one will be listening when you start your whining because this time you've gone too far.'

'For God's sake!' I mumbled to Jamie, who was staring into space. 'Say something.'

'Don't expect him to say anything,' Bob said.

'Jamie?'

'What did I tell you?' Bob said, pushing back his chair.

'You don't believe that, do you, that *we* killed him?' I said, plaintively.

'You're wasting your breath. Of course he believes it. They all do,' Bob said. 'Come on, let's go. We don't belong here.'

I shrugged off the hand on my shoulder, and turned to Jamie, waiting for some kind of reaction, but when he refused to look at me I found myself rising to my feet and following Bob through the door.

Outside, the cold air hit me like a slap. Peering at

his watch, Bob suggested another drink, and without thinking or speaking I followed him into a pub. I knew I wanted to say something, but whether from shock or anger, no words would come. Finally, breaking the silence, Bob said: 'Don't look so bloody surprised.'

'It was the way he wouldn't look at me. I could see him thinking "Bloody Yid".'

'Probably.'

'After all these years! I mean, not nowadays ... fifty years ago, of course, nothing would have surprised me ... but Jamie!'

'Nothing's changed.'

'Look, my hands are shaking!' I said.

'Better have another drink.'

'I'm serious.'

'So am I.'

'You know,' I said, after we'd found an empty booth and sat down, 'I've known him a long time, yet still had no idea. From Duncan, yes, of course, I always expected something snide, he couldn't help it, but not the Wilkinsons. When I was with them, I almost forgot I was a Jew.'

'You didn't want to know, that's all. You never have.'

I stared at Bob with a mixture of fury and gratitude. What did he know about friendship, love...? Perhaps more than I'd ever given him credit for.

'You know,' I said, 'before you arrived I had a funny thought. Seeing that empty chair reminded me of Passover.'

'And instead of the prophet Elijah, I turned up!'

'I don't know what I'd have done if you hadn't been there.'

'You'd have had a nice, quiet evening, with no fuss and be in bed by now.'

'He just sat there, not saying a word.'

'What did you expect?'

'Something ... I don't know ... anything.'

'He's weak, he was embarrassed. He didn't want anyone to spoil his precious dinner party, and we ruined it for him. Clumsy, ill-mannered Jews with big mouths who don't know how to behave.'

'Speak for yourself,' I said, trying not to smile.

The bell rang for last orders, and I took our glasses to the bar. As we were leaving I said: 'What do you think was the point of it all? I mean, he went to all that trouble and expense and for what? He didn't want anyone to say a word, certainly not to hear the truth about Duncan.'

'What that *schmuck* said, in a way he's right. We've lost our moral authority. Not that they give a shit about the Arabs. They're just grateful to be off the hook after all this time.'

'That's what my old man thinks. But what I can't understand is why anyone expects Jews to behave differently from other people, not after centuries of oppression and all that. ... Now we're behaving like them, they no longer have a victim.'

'The English have always expected people to take it lying down.'

'It's called the missionary position!'

'People always find someone to have a go at. Sooner or later it'll be our turn again.'

'Sometimes I think Israel won't be happy until it's got the whole world against it,' I said.

We staggered arm in arm towards The Mall. Bob was now in a playful mood and more than likely I'd have to stop him pulling faces at the guardsmen outside the Palace. After we'd been walking for a while I said: 'What on earth was he trying to prove, having us all there as his guests?'

'How should I know? He's *your* friend.'

'Was,' I said. 'Was.'

'You'll make it up, I expect. He probably doesn't think anything's happened.'

'He knows all right.'

'Have it your own way,' he said. Then, staring up at the Victoria memorial, he added, out of the blue, '*Goyim nachas*. That's all it was.'

It was a derogatory Yiddish expression, meaning literally 'Gentile pleasures', which my father used to denigrate the things I admired most about England. But it was not really translatable, part of the private language of a people who for centuries had been trying hard not to be understood.

'What is?' I asked.

'All the palaver. That nonsense with the port.'

'You know, I couldn't believe he was serious. What the fuck difference does it make which way you pass the bottle – sorry – decanter? Pompous ass!'

175

'He was perfectly serious. That's what was so funny. Only he couldn't see it.'

'Still, you don't think we went a bit far? That stuff about Duncan's love-life was below the belt. We were supposed to be his friends, after all.'

It was a warm night, and as I gazed at the low, light clouds scudding across the sky and the flood-lit facade of the Palace, I realised I was feeling relaxed for the first time that evening. 'Yes,' I said, 'you're right. It was just *Goyim nachas* ... Speaking of which, I see Queenie's safely tucked up in bed.'

Bob put on his most serious face. Then we both began to laugh.